The Secret of Cliff Castle and Other Stories

The Secret of Cliff Castle
Enid Blyton
Illustrations by Kevin Kimber

The Children of Kidillin
Enid Blyton
Illustrations by Patricia Ludlow

Smuggler Ben
Enid Blyton
Illustrations by Paul Fisher Johnson

BLOOMSBURY
CHILDREN'S
BOOKS

First published by Parragon Publishing in 1999
Queen Street House, 4/5 Queen Street, Bath BA1 1HE

The Secret of Cliff Castle was first published by T. Werner Laurie Ltd in 1947
The Children of Kidillin was first published by Newnes in 1940
Smuggler Ben was first published by T. Werner Laurie Ltd in 1943
First published by Bloomsbury Publishing Plc in 1997
38 Soho Square, London, W1V 5DF

Enid Blyton

The moral right of the author has been asserted
A CIP catalogue record of this book is available from the
British Library

ISBN 1 84164 096 4

Printed in Scotland by Caledonian International Book Manufacturing Ltd

10 9 8 7 6 5 4 3 2 1

Cover Design by Mandy Sherliker

Contents

The Secret of
Cliff Castle

The Secret of Cliff Castle

Enid Blyton
Illustrations by Kevin Kimber

BLOOMSBURY
CHILDREN'S
BOOKS

Contents

CHAPTER 1

OFF FOR A HOLIDAY

Peter and Pam leaned out of the railway carriage together and waved goodbye to their mother as their train slowly left the long platform.

'Goodbye, Mother! Goodbye!'

'Be good!' called Mother. 'Goodbye! Have a lovely holiday! Give my love to Auntie Hetty.'

'I hope Brock will be at the station to meet us,' said Peter. 'Good old Brock. It will be lovely to see his round, smiling face again.'

Brock was their cousin. They were going to stay with him for part of the summer holidays, down in the country village of Rockhurst. Usually they went to the sea, but this summer Mother thought it would be nice for them to be in the country. Then Auntie Hetty had written to invite them for three weeks, and the children had been thrilled.

'We can go to the farm and see all the new animals there,' said Pam. 'And we can go exploring in the woods and find exciting things there. I hope there are some woods near.'

'There are always woods in the country,' said Peter. 'Anyway, Brock will know all the places to go to. It's fun going to a place we've never been to before!'

The train sped on. It soon left London behind, and green fields took the place of houses and streets. The train was an express, and stopped at very few stations. The children had sandwiches with them, and when Pam's wristwatch showed half-past twelve, Peter undid the parcel Mother had handed them, and took out the packets of food.

'I always feel so hungry in a train, somehow,' said Pam. 'Oooh – ham sandwiches. How lovely! What's in that other packet, Peter?'

'Biscuits, and two pieces of cake,' said Peter, looking to see. 'Oh, and two bars of chocolate as well. What a nice lunch. Mother's put in some lemonade, too – it's in that bag, Pam. Get it down.'

Pam reached down the leather bag, in which Mother had squeezed a bottle of lemonade and two cardboard cups. Soon the two children were eating a lovely lunch, watching the scenery as it flew by the carriage window.

'We shall arrive at Rockhurst at half-past three,' said Peter. 'But we've got to change at Deane. We must look out for that.'

It was quite easy to change at Deane. A porter came by, calling, 'Change here for Rockhurst! Change here for Rockhurst,' and out the children hopped with their suitcases. The little train for Rockhurst stood on the other side of the platform, and they simply got out of one train and into the other! It was fun.

'Shan't be long now,' said Peter. 'You know, Pam, I feel awfully excited. I feel as if we're going to have adventures!'

'I feel that too,' said Pam. 'But I usually do feel like that when I'm setting out on a holiday.'

'So do I,' said Peter. 'But this time I feel we really are. Proper adventures, I mean. Sort of dangerous, you know!'

'Do you really?' said Pam, feeling all excited too. 'Oooh, I hope we do have some. I'd like some. School was so dull last term that I could do with something exciting in the hols!'

'Goodness! Isn't it slow, after the express!' said Pam. 'We could almost lean out of the window and pick flowers off the bank!'

Peter laughed. 'Well, in another twenty minutes we shall be there,' he said. 'And then we'll see old Brock.'

The time went by, and at exactly half-past

three the little train drew in at a small country platform, where red geraniums flared in beds at the back. 'Rockhurst!' shouted the one and only porter. 'Rockhurst!'

Peter jumped out, and helped Pam down. She looked eagerly up and down the platform, whilst Peter dragged out the two suitcases and the big leather bag. Pam gave a shriek.

'Oh! There's Brock! Brock! Brock! Here we are! Hello!'

Brock came rushing up. He was a tall boy, with a strong body, and a red, smiling face. His eyes shone very blue in the sunshine as he greeted his cousins. He was twelve, the same age as Peter, but stronger and taller. Pam was eleven, smaller than either of the boys.

Brock clapped his cousins on the back, and grinned at them. 'Hello! Glad to see you both! Welcome to Rockhurst!'

'Hello!' said Peter, smiling. 'It's fine to see you, Brock. Gosh, you've grown awfully tall since we saw you last year. You make me feel quite small.'

'Come on,' said Brock, taking one of the suitcases. 'Mother's outside with the pony-cart. It'll just about take us all, though we'll have to put our feet on these cases.'

They gave up their tickets, and went out of the station, chattering hard. Pam called out to

her aunt, in delight, 'Hello, Aunt Hetty! Here we are! It *is* nice of you to come and meet us.'

'Hello, my dears,' said their aunt. 'Glad to see you. Climb into the cart. Brock, hand up the cases first, and I'll pack them under our feet.'

Soon the four of them were driving swiftly along the country lanes. Sally, the pony, was a smart little beast, and cantered along merrily. The sun shone down, and everything looked bright and holiday-like. The children felt very happy.

They soon arrived at Brock's home. It was a comfortable-looking house, rather rambling, set in a nice big garden. The children liked the look of it very much.

'It's a friendly sort of house, isn't it?' said Pam. 'Oh, Aunt Hetty, isn't the beginning of a holiday exciting?'

'Very exciting!' said their aunt. 'Quite the most exciting part of a holiday, I always think.'

'But it isn't going to be the most exciting part of *this* holiday!' said Peter, as the pony trotted in at the gate and came to a standstill in front of the house. 'I've got a funny feeling about this holiday. It's going to be exciting all the way through!'

'What do you mean?' asked Brock in surprise.

'I don't exactly know,' said Peter, jumping down, and helping his aunt out. 'But I've got a feeling! You just wait and see!'

'Well, I hope your feeling is right!' said Brock, and they all went into the house.

CHAPTER 2
A LITTLE EXPLORING

Tea was ready when they got indoors. The children washed their hands and brushed their hair. Peter was sharing Brock's little room, and Pam had a tiny room to herself up in the attic. She loved it because it had peculiar, slanting ceilings, and funny, uneven boards in the floor. She looked out of the window as she brushed her hair, humming a little tune to herself because she was so happy.

The countryside lay smiling in the afternoon sunshine. Cottages clustered together here and there, and cattle grazed in the fields. In the distance, a curious, steep hill caught her eye. It rose up very suddenly, and at the top was a strange building. It looked like a small, square castle, for it had towers at each end.

'I wonder if anyone lives there,' thought Pam.

'It looks sort of deserted, somehow. I'll ask Brock about it.'

Downstairs, round the tea table, Brock and his cousins chattered nineteen to the dozen about everything, telling each other all their news. Aunt Hetty smiled as she listened, and handed round her plates of home-made scones with jam, and new ginger buns, and currant pasties.

'Anyone would think you hadn't had anything to eat since breakfast-time,' she said, as one after another the plates were emptied.

'Well, we did have a good lunch on the train,' said Peter, 'but it seems ages ago now. I do like these buns, Aunt Hetty. They're the nicest I've ever tasted.'

'Shall we go out and explore round a bit, after tea?' said Pam. 'I'm longing to. I saw the farm not far off, Brock – and what is that strange sort of castle on the top of that very steep hill towards the west?'

'Oh, that's Cliff Castle,' said Brock. 'It's called that because it's built on that steep hill, which falls away behind the castle in a kind of cliff.'

'Does anyone live there?' asked Peter.

'Not now,' said Brock. 'Mother, who lived there, years ago?'

'Oh, I don't really know,' said Mother. 'It belonged to a strange old man who wanted to live quite alone. So he built himself that castle, and lived there with two old servants, as strange as himself. He spent a fortune on the castle. When he died, he left a will which said the castle was to be left exactly as it was, cared for by the two old servants till they died. Then it was to go to some great-nephew, who has never bothered to live there – or even to go and visit the castle, as far as I know.'

'Is it really a castle?' said Pam.

'No, not really,' said Aunt Hetty. 'But it's built to appear like one, as you see – and I believe the walls are almost as thick as a real old castle's would be. People do say that there are secret passages in it, but I don't believe that. What would a lonely old man want with secret passages! That's just make believe.'

The children stared out of the window at the lonely castle on the top of the steep hill. It suddenly seemed very mysterious and exciting to them. It stood there, with the sinking sun behind it, and looked rather black and forbidding.

'Is it quite empty then, Aunt Hetty?' asked Pam.

'Quite,' said her aunt. 'It must be a dreadful mess by now, too, I should think, for nobody has dusted it for years, or lit a fire there to warm the place. The furniture must be mouldy and rotten. Not a nice place to visit at all!'

Peter and Pam looked at one another. It seemed to them that their aunt was quite wrong. It would be a wonderfully exciting place to visit! If only they could!

After tea, they spoke to Brock about it. 'Brock! Will you take us to see Cliff Castle one day soon? Tomorrow, perhaps. It does sound so exciting – and it looks so strange and lonely. We'd simply love to explore round about it.'

'We'll go tomorrow!' said Brock. 'But come and see our garden now – and the farm. We've plenty of time.'

So the three of them went over to Brock's big garden, and admired the vegetables, the outdoor tomatoes, the peaches on the wall, and everything. They saw Brock's exciting playhouse in the garden, too, set all by itself out of sight of the house.

'Daddy had this built for me to take my friends to, when we wanted to play by ourselves,' said Brock. 'You know, Mother doesn't like a lot of noise, and boys can't help being rowdy, can they? So I just take my friends to my playhouse when we want a good old game – and we don't disturb Mother a bit! We can play out here on rainy days, too. It will be fun.'

Peter and Pam liked Brock's playhouse. It was a small, sturdy, little wooden house with a red door, and windows each side. Inside there was

one big room, and around it were spread all Brock's possessions – a small record player, a big Meccano set, boxes and boxes of railway lines, engines, trucks, signals, and other things belonging to a railway – and on a bookshelf were scores of exciting-looking books.

'You *are* lucky, Brock!' said Peter, looking round. 'This is a lovely place.'

'Yes – we'll come here and talk when we want to be all by ourselves,' said Brock. 'Nobody can see us or hear us. It's our own private place.'

They went to see the farm, too – and then the sun sank so low that it was time to go back home to supper. The strange castle on the hill showed up clearly as they went down the farm lane back to their house.

'Brock, do take us to Cliff Castle tomorrow,' said Peter. 'It would be marvellous fun to explore it. Haven't you ever been there yourself?'

'I haven't been very near it,' said Brock. 'I somehow never liked the look of it very much, you know. I think it's got rather a wicked look!'

'It has, rather,' said Peter. 'Anyway, do let's go tomorrow!'

'All right,' said Brock. 'I shan't mind going with you – though I've never wanted to go alone!'

It was fun going to bed that night in a strange bedroom. The two boys talked till late, and

Brock's mother had to go in twice to stop them. Pam could hear their voices as she lay in bed, and she wished she was with the two boys so that she might hear what they said.

She fell asleep, and did not wake until the house was all in a bustle with its early morning cleaning. She heard the two boys talking below in loud voices, and she jumped out of bed at once.

'It's holiday-time – and we're at Brock's – and we're going exploring today!' she hummed to herself, as she dressed quickly. She ran down-stairs to breakfast feeling very hungry.

'What are you going to do today?' asked Aunt Hetty, pouring out the tea.

'We're going over to Cliff Castle,' said Brock. 'Can we take sandwiches, Mother, and have a picnic?'

'All right,' said his mother. 'You must all make your beds, and tidy your rooms, please, before you go. I'll get you some lunch ready whilst you do that.'

It wasn't long after breakfast before the three children were ready to set out. Brock's mother had been very generous with the picnic lunch. She had cut them meat sandwiches, tomato sand-wiches, and egg sandwiches, and had put some buttered scones, some ginger buns, and some boiled sweets into the packets, too.

'There's a tiny shop, not far from Cliff Castle, where you can buy yourselves something to drink,' she said. 'Here is some money for that. Now – off you go!'

They set off happily. Brock knew the way, though it was rather a roundabout one, down narrow little lanes, through a small wood, and then across some fields. It was eleven o'clock by the time they got to the little shop where they wanted to buy drinks.

'I'm so thirsty already that I could drink about twelve bottles of lemonade straight off!' said Peter.

'Well, don't let's drink all of it straightaway,' said Brock. 'The woman here has a well – look, there it is, with the bucket beside it. Let's ask her if we can have a drink of cold water – then we can save up the lemonade!'

The woman said that of course they could use her well water. 'Have a whole bucketful, if you like!' she said. But they couldn't quite manage that. They sent down the bucket, and it came up filled with silvery water.

'It's absolutely ice-cold!' said Pam, gasping a little at the coldness. 'But it's simply lovely.'

'Where are you off to?' asked the woman, handing out three small bottles of lemonade.

'To explore round about Cliff Castle,' said Peter.

'Oh, I wouldn't do that,' said the woman. 'Really, I wouldn't. It's a strange place. And people do say that funny lights have been seen there lately. Well, that's very strange, isn't it, in a place that's been empty for years?'

'Most peculiar,' said Brock, staring at the woman, and feeling rather excited. 'What sort of lights?'

'I don't know,' said the woman. 'I only know I wouldn't go near that place in the dark, or in the daytime either! There's always been something odd about it – and there is still!'

The children said goodbye and went out of the tiny, dark shop. They stared up at the nearby hill, on the top of which stood Cliff Castle. It looked much bigger now that they were near it. It had funny little slit-like windows, just like very old castles had. It certainly was a peculiar place for anyone to build in days when castles were no longer of any use!

'Well, come on,' said Brock, at last. 'Don't let's be put off by silly village stories. Mother says stories always get made up about any deserted place.'

'They certainly make it more exciting,' said Peter hitching his kitbag full of lunch over his shoulder. 'Well – up the hill we go!'

And up the hill they went. There was no proper road up the steep hill, only a small, narrow path that wound between jutting-out rocks, for it was a very rocky part of the countryside. Stunted bushes grew on the hillside, mostly of gorse. It was exposed to the east winds, and nothing very much grew there.

'Well – here we are!' said Brock, at last. 'Cliff Castle! I wonder what we shall find there?'

CHAPTER 3
CLIFF CASTLE

Now that the children were right up to the castle, it looked enormous! It rose up in front of them, square and sturdy, a tower at each end. Its small, slit-like windows had no glass in. The great front door was studded with big nails that had gone rusty. There was a large knocker, which the children longed to use – but which, of course, they dared not touch!

'Let's go all the way round the castle and see what we can see,' said Pam.

So they went down the great flight of steps again, and began to make their way round the towering walls of the strange castle. It was difficult, because creepers, bushes and weeds grew high up the walls. Tall nettles stood in great patches, and the children had to make their way round them after Pam was badly stung on her bare legs.

'We'll find some dock leaves to help the stings,' said Peter, and he found a patch of dark green dock leaves. He picked some and Pam pressed the cool leaves against her burning skin.

'That's better,' she said. 'Gracious, I shan't go near nettles again today!'

They went on their way round the great grey walls. The slit-like windows were placed at regular intervals. The children gazed up at them.

'You know, in the olden days, they had those funny narrow windows so that archers could shoot their arrows out without being hit themselves,' said Brock rather learnedly. 'I can't imagine why the old man should have built windows like that for himself, long after the time of bows and arrows had gone! It must make the rooms inside very dark.'

'I wish we could see them, don't you?' said Pam excitedly. 'Just imagine how strange they would look after all these years when nobody has been here – cobwebs all over the place – dust everywhere. Oooh – it would be very odd.'

They could not go all round the castle, because, when they came to the side that faced due west, the hill fell away so steeply that it was impossible to go any further. The walls of the castle were built almost sheer with the hillside, and there was a very big drop down to the bottom of the hills below.

'Let's have our lunch now,' said Peter, all at once feeling terribly hungry. 'It's almost time. We can find a nice place out of the hot sun and sit down, can't we?'

'Rather!' said Brock, feeling hungry too. 'Look – what about that shady bit over there, facing the castle? We can look at the castle whilst we're eating.'

They sat down in the shady spot, and undid all they had to eat. It had seemed a lot when Brock's mother had packed it up – but it didn't seem nearly so much when three hungry children began to eat it. They unscrewed the tops of the lemonade bottles, and drank eagerly. Except that the lemonade tasted a little warm, it was delicious.

Pam finished her lunch first, because she did not want so much as the boys, and gave some of hers to them to finish up. She lay back against a tree and looked up at the silent grey castle.

She looked at the narrow windows and began to count them. When she came to the second row, she spoke out loud: 'Look, Peter; look, Brock – there's a window in the second row up that is bigger than the others. I wonder why.'

The boys looked up. Peter screwed up his eyes to see why the window should be bigger.

'I don't think it's meant to be bigger,' he said, at last. 'I think the weather has sort of eaten it away. It looks to me as if the bottom part of it has crumbled away. Perhaps a pipe comes out just there, and has leaked down the window and made the stone and brickwork rotten.'

'Do you see the tree that grows up to that window?' said Brock, in sudden excitement. 'I believe we could climb it and look in at that window! I wonder what we should see if we did!'

Peter and Pam stared at him, and then at the tree that grew up to the window. What fun it would be if they really could climb it and have a peep inside the castle!

'Well, let's see if we can peep inside any of the lower windows first,' said Peter. 'I don't think Aunt Hetty would be very pleased with us if we climbed trees in these clothes. We really want old clothes for that.'

'Oh, bother our clothes!' said Brock, his red face shining with excitement. 'I vote we climb up! But we'll have a peep in at one of the lower windows first. Peter, you come and give me a leg up.'

It wasn't long before Peter was bending down, heaving Brock up to the narrow window-sill to see inside the slit-like window. Brock peered through, but could see nothing at all.

'It's so dark inside,' he said. 'It wouldn't be so bad if the sun wasn't so brilliant today – but my eyes just simply can't see a thing inside the darkness of the castle.'

'Well, we'll climb the tree then!' cried Pam, running to it. She loved climbing trees as much as the boys did.

'Wait a bit, Pam,' cried Brock. 'Peter and I will go up first, and give you a hand. You're only a girl, you know.'

It always made Pam cross to be told she was only a girl. 'I'm as strong as you are, anyway!' she cried, and looked about for an easy way to climb.

But Brock was up the tree before either of the others. He was a country boy, used to climbing, and he saw at once the best way to go up. He was soon lost to sight among the greenery.

His voice came down to them: 'Go up the way I did. It's not difficult.'

Peter followed him, and then Pam. Pam had to have a hand from Peter every now and again, and she was glad of it. They were soon all of them up on a high branch beside Brock. He grinned at them.

'Good climbing!' he said. 'Now, look – see this branch? It reaches right to that window. It's pretty strong, and I think it will bear us all. But we'd better go one at a time, in case it doesn't.'

'You go first, then,' said Peter. Brock edged his way along the branch, working carefully with his arms and legs. The bough bent beneath his weight and swung down below the window-sill. Brock came back.

'No good,' he said. 'We'll try the next branch. That looks a good deal stronger – and although it grows right above the window at its tip, our weight will bend it down till it rests almost on the window-sill, I should think.'

They all climbed a little higher. Then Brock worked his way along the next branch. As he said, his weight bent it gradually down, and by the time he was at the end of it, its tip rested on the sill itself. Part of it even went right through the window-opening into the castle.

'Fine!' said Brock. He put one leg across the stone window-sill, and peered into the slit. He could see nothing but darkness. But certainly the weather had worn away the stone around that window, for the opening was almost big enough to take Brock's stout body!

'I believe I could get right inside!' he called to the others. He stood upright on the sill and tried to work his way in. It was a very tight fit, for Brock was not thin! He had to squeeze himself in till he almost burst.

He found that the wall was very thick – about a yard thick, before he had got right through the window. Then he jumped down to the floor inside and called out through the slit: 'Come on! It's not very difficult! We'll be able to explore the castle from top to bottom, if you can get through!'

CHAPTER 4

INSIDE THE CASTLE

Pam felt a little nervous about going right into the castle, but she couldn't hold back if the boys thought it was all right. So she followed Peter when he squeezed himself through the slit in the stone walls, and held his hand tightly when he gave it to her to jump down into the darkness.

Two slit-like windows lighted the room they were in. It seemed as dark as night to the children when they first looked round – but their eyes soon grew accustomed to it, and they began to see quite well. Shafts of bright sunlight lit up the room in two places – the rest seemed rather dark.

They stared round, and then Pam cried out in disappointment: 'Oh – the room is empty! It's just like a prison cell! There's absolutely nothing here!'

She was right. There was nothing to see at all, except for bare walls, bare floor, and bare ceiling. At the far side was a closed door, big and strong. It had an iron handle. Brock went over to it.

'Well, we may be unlucky in this room, finding nothing to see,' he said, 'but maybe there will be plenty to see somewhere else! Let's open this door and explore!'

He pulled at the door by the great iron handle. It opened! Outside was a dark passage. Brock felt in his pockets, remembering that he had a torch somewhere. He found it, and switched it on.

The passage led from a narrow stone stairway, and seemed to wind round a corner. 'Come on,' said Brock. 'This way! We'll open a few doors and see what there is to be seen.'

He opened a door nearby. But again there was nothing to be seen but bareness. He shut the door, and the noise echoed through the stone castle in a very strange way. It sounded as though dozens of doors were being shut, one after another. Pam shivered.

'Oooh!' she said. 'It's not nice to make a noise in this place. Even a little sound echoes round like thunder.'

No room just there had anything in it at all. It was most disappointing. Brock then led the way to the stone staircase. It wound downwards in the heart of the castle, and as it came towards the bottom, grew a little wider.

It ended in a vast room with an enormous fireplace at one end. 'This must be the kitchen,' said Pam in surprise. 'And I suppose those stairs we came down were the back stairs. There must be a bigger flight somewhere else. I did think they were very narrow stairs for such a huge castle.'

The kitchen was furnished. There was a big wooden table, and around it were set stout wooden chairs. Pots and pans hung around the stove. There was an iron pot hanging over what had once been a fire. Brock peered into it. There was an evil-smelling, dark liquid in it.

'Something made by witches!' he said, in a deep, mournful voice that made Pam jump. Brock laughed. 'It's all right,' he said. 'It's only some soup, or something gone bad after all these years!'

The kitchen was dark and dirty, and there was not much to be seen there. The children went out of it and came into a great hall from which four doors led off. Brock opened one.

And then, indeed, there was something to be seen! The big room beyond the door was furnished most magnificently! Great couches, carved chairs, cabinets, tables — all these stood about the room just as they had been left! But how mournful they looked, for they were adorned with great spiders' webs, and when the children walked into the room, clouds of fine grey dust flew up from their feet.

Sunlight came in long golden shafts through four of the slit-like windows, and divided the room into quarters. It made the whole room even stranger than it might have been, for the brilliance of the sunlight lay in sharp contrast to the blackness of the shadows in the far corners.

'Oooh! What an enormous spider!' said Pam, with a shudder, as a great eight-legged spider ran out from under a table. The boys didn't mind spiders. They didn't even mind walking into the cobwebs that hung here and there from the enormous chandeliers that had once held dozens of candles to light the room. But Pam couldn't bear the strange, light touch of the webs on her hair, and longed to get out into the sunshine again.

'Isn't it odd, to have left everything just like this?' said Brock wonderingly. 'Look at those curtains. They must once have been simply gorgeous – but now they are all faded and dusty.'

He touched one – and it fell to pieces in his hand. It was almost as if someone had breathed on it and made it melt!

'The brocade on the furniture is all rotten, too,' said Pam, as she felt it. It shredded away under her fingers. 'Everything is moth-eaten.

What a horrid, sad place this feels. I don't like it. Let's get away.'

'No – we'll explore first,' said Peter. 'Don't be a spoilsport, Pam. Come with us. You'll be quite all right.'

Pam didn't want to be a spoilsport, so she followed the boys rather unwillingly as they went out of the room and into the next.

The same things were found there – furniture and curtains, rotten and decayed. A musty smell hung over everything. It was most unpleasant. Pam began to feel sick.

'I hate this smell,' she said, 'and I hate walking into these horrid webs. I can't seem to see them and it's horrid to get them all round my head.'

'Let's go upstairs again,' said Brock. 'And this time we'll go up by the main stairway – look, that great flight of steps over there – not by the little narrow back staircase we came down.'

They mounted the enormous stone steps, and came to some big rooms furnished as bedrooms. Up they went again and came to more rooms. Leading out of one of them was a tiny staircase all on its own. It wound up into one of the stone towers that stood at the end of the castle.

'Let's go up this staircase!' cried Peter. 'We shall get a marvellous view over the countryside!'

So up they went and came to the open door of a strange, square little room that seemed to be cut right out of the heart of the tower. A tiny slit on each side lighted it. A stone bench ran round the walls, but otherwise there was nothing in the room.

'What a wonderful view!' cried Pam, peering out of one of the slits. She saw the whole of the countryside to the east lying smiling in the hot August sun. It looked marvellous.

'I can see our house!' cried Brock. 'Over there, beyond the farm. Oh, how tiny it looks! And how small the cows and horses look, too. Like animals on a toy farm.'

So they did. It was fun to peer out and see everything from so high up. But soon the children grew tired of it and thought they would go downstairs again.

So down they went, and then paused on the first floor where they had first squeezed in through the window. But somehow they couldn't find the room they had climbed inside! It was strange. They opened door after door, but no, there wasn't a tree outside a window.

'I've lost my bearings,' said Peter, at last. 'I've no idea where that room was. Well, if we don't want to stay here all night we've got to get out somehow! I vote we go right downstairs into the hall, then make our way to the kitchen, and up that back stairway again. We know the room was somewhere near the top of that.'

So down they went, into the hall, into the kitchen, and then towards the back stairway.

But just near the stairway was a small door, very low, set in the wall. The children stared at it. They hadn't noticed it before.

'Perhaps we could open this and get out by it,' said Peter. 'It would save us all that big climb down the tree. I tried the front door to see if we could get out by that, but it was much too heavy. The bolts had all rusted into the door, and I couldn't even turn the handle. Let's try this funny little door.'

'It's so low we'll have to bend down to get out of it!' said Brock, with a laugh. They went to the little door and looked at it. It was latched on the inside, but not bolted or locked, though the key stood in the door. Peter lifted the latch.

After a push, the door opened a little way, and then stuck fast. The two boys together pushed hard. It opened just a little further, and sunshine came through.

Peter put his head round the edge. 'There's a great patch of nettles and a gorse bush preventing it from opening,' he said. 'Got a knife, Brock? I believe if I hacked away at this gorse bush a bit I could make the door open enough to let us out!'

Brock passed him a fierce-looking knife. Peter hacked at the bush, and cut off the pieces that were stopping the door from opening.

'Cut away the nettles, too,' begged Pam. 'My legs still sting from that other patch we went into.'

Peter did his best. Then he and Brock were able to push the door open just enough to let them squeeze through one by one. They were all rather glad to be standing out in the bright sunshine again, after the dim, musty darkness of the silent castle.

'I say – if we just push this door to, and leave it like that, not locked or bolted, we shall be able to get in whenever we want to!' said Peter. 'We might find it rather fun to come and play smugglers or something here. We could pile weeds against the door so that nobody else would notice it.'

'Good idea!' said Brock. So they shut the door gently, then forced the gorse bush back against it, and pulled pieces from a nearby hedge to throw against the door to hide it.

Pam got stung again by the nettles, and almost cried with the pain. Peter had to hunt for dock leaves again!

'Cheer up!' he said. 'What do a few nettle-stings matter? We've had quite an adventure this afternoon! We'll come back here again soon and have a fine time.'

Pam wasn't sure she wanted to. But she didn't say so! The boys talked eagerly about the afternoon's excitement on the way home – and by the time they reached the house, Pam had begun to think that nettle-stings or no nettle-stings, it had all been simply marvellous!

CHAPTER 5

IN THE MIDDLE
OF THE NIGHT

The next day Aunt Hetty took Pam and Peter and their cousin Brock in the pony-cart to the sea, which was about three miles away. This was such fun that the three children forgot all about Cliff Castle for a day or two. And then something happened that reminded them of it.

It was something that happened in the middle of the night. Pam woke up and felt very thirsty. She remembered that Aunt Hetty had left a jug of water and a tumbler on the mantelpiece and she got up to get it.

She stood at the window, drinking the water. It was a moonlit night, but the moon kept going behind clouds. It showed up Cliff Castle very clearly, when it shone down. But when it went behind the clouds the castle was just a black mass on the hill.

Then Pam saw something flickering quickly

somewhere at the top of the castle. It caught her eye for a second and then disappeared. What could it be?

She stood watching the castle, forgetting to drink the cool water. Then the flicker came again, this time further down the castle. Then it disappeared once more. It came for the third and last time at the bottom.

Pam felt excited. She remembered what the woman at the little shop had said about strange lights being seen in the castle. Now here they were again – and they were real, because Pam had seen them!

'I really must wake the boys and tell them!' she thought. 'I know it isn't a dream now – but in the morning I might think it was, and not tell them. But it isn't a dream, I've seen the lights!'

She crept down the stairs and into the open door of the boys' room. They were both sleeping peacefully. Pam shook Peter and he woke with a jump.

'What is it?' he said loudly, sitting up in bed, surprised to see that it was night.

'Sh!' said Pam. 'It's me, Peter. Listen – I got up to get a drink of water – and I saw lights in Cliff Castle!'

'Gosh!' said Peter, jumping out of bed and going to the window. 'Did you really? I say – let's wake Brock.'

But Brock was already awake, disturbed by the noise. He was soon told what the matter was, and went to the window, too. All three watched for a little time — and then, suddenly, a light flickered again, this time at the bottom of the castle.

'There it is!' said Pam, clutching Peter and making him jump almost out of his skin. 'Did you see it?'

'Of course,' said Peter. 'And there it is again — the first floor somewhere this time — and there again, higher up — and now it's right at the very top. Somewhere in that tower, look. It's the very tower we were in the other day!'

Pam felt a bit frightened. Who could be in the castle so late at night? The children watched for a little longer and then went back to bed, puzzled and excited.

'I vote we go there tomorrow again, and see if there's anyone there,' said Brock. Nothing ever frightened Brock, and nothing ever stopped him from smiling! He meant to find out the secret of Cliff Castle as soon as possible!

So the next day three excited children met in Brock's playhouse in the garden to discuss their plans. They all felt certain that somebody was living in, or visiting, the castle — someone who had no right to be there. Who could it be — and why did he go there?

'When can we go?' asked Peter eagerly.

'After dinner,' said Brock. 'We're going over to the market this morning, in the next town. We don't want to miss that. It's fun. Dad will take us in his car.'

So it was not until after the three children had been to the market, and had come back and eaten a most enormous dinner that they set off to Cliff Castle once again.

They stopped at the little shop where once before they had bought lemonade. The woman served them again with sweet drinks, which they drank in the shop.

'Any more been heard about the lights in Cliff Castle?' they asked the woman, when they paid her. She shook her head.

'Not that I know of,' she said. 'But don't you go wandering about there, my dears. It's a dangerous place.'

They went off again, and soon came near the castle, which towered above them on its hill. They climbed the hill by the narrow rocky path and came to the big flight of overgrown stone steps.

'We won't go up the steps, in case there really is somebody in the castle, watching,' said Peter. 'We'll try and find that tiny little door. You know – the one we left latched.'

So they made their way around nettle patches

and other weeds until they came to where the little low door was set in the thick stone walls. The branches they had pulled from the nearby hedge were still against it. Nobody had disturbed them.

They pulled at the door, lifting the iron latch as they did so. It opened silently, and the children squeezed through, shutting it after them. They stood in the big kitchen, so dark and musty, shining their torches all around.

There was nothing new to be seen. They crossed the kitchen and went out into the hall – and here Brock gave a cry of surprise, and levelled his torch steadily on something on the ground.

The others looked. Pam couldn't make out why Brock was so excited, because all she saw were footprints crossing and recrossing the floor – and, after all, they had all walked there themselves last time!

'What's the matter?' she said.

'Can't you see, silly?' said Peter, pointing to a set of footprints that went across the floor. 'Look at those. Those are not our marks. None of us have feet as big as that, and certainly we don't wear boots studded with nails. You can see the mark the nails have made in the thick dust.'

Pam and the others stared at the marks. Yes – it was quite plain that somebody grown-up had walked across that floor. Brock found another track and shone his torch on it.

'*Two* men have been here,' he said thoughtfully. 'Look – this set of prints shows a narrower foot than the other. Now, I wonder whatever two men were doing here?'

The children stared at one another. They couldn't imagine why men should visit the castle in the middle of the night. Perhaps they had come to steal something?

'Let's look in the rooms down here and see if anything has been disturbed,' said Brock, at last. So they opened the nearest door and looked into the room there, still festooned with cobwebs, and still smelling of the same horrid, musty smell.

'Nothing has been moved,' said Brock. 'And there are only *our* footprints here. No one else's. Let's follow these other prints and see where they go. They show very clearly, don't they?'

They did show clearly in the thick dust. It was fairly easy to sort them out from the tracks the children themselves had made, for the men's prints were large and had made more impression in the dust. The children followed the prints up the big stairway to the first floor. There, neatly outlined in the dust, was something else!

'Look at that big oblong shape marked in the dust!' said Brock. 'It looks as if someone had put down a big box there, doesn't it?'

'Yes,' said Peter. 'And look – there's the mark of another box, or something, further along. It looks as if the men had been carrying something very heavy up the stairs, and had put their load down for a rest before going on. See how their footprints are muddled here, too, as if they had picked up their load again and gone on carrying further along.'

'I feel rather like a detective!' said Pam excitedly. 'Tracking things like this! I wonder where the men took their loads to! I expect that explains the lights we saw last night. The men had torches, and every time they passed one of those slit-like windows, the reflection shone out for a moment, like a flicker. I guess they didn't know that!'

'Come on,' said Brock impatiently. 'Let's follow on.'

They went on, past many closed doors and up another flight of stone steps. This brought them to the second floor. The footprints still went on!

'I believe they're going up to that tower!' said Pam. 'We saw the light flicker there, you know. Oh – I hope the men aren't hiding there!'

This made the boys stop hurriedly. They hadn't thought of that! Suppose somebody was up there in the tower? That wouldn't be very pleasant, because they would be sure to be angry to see children interfering.

'We'd better go very quietly indeed, and not speak a word!' said Brock in a whisper. 'Come on.'

So in complete silence, their hearts beating fast, the three children crept on and up until they came to the room where the little stone staircase led up into the tower. They mounted it quietly, seeing the men's footprints still on the steps.

They came to the wooden door that had been open the first time they had gone up the staircase. This time it was shut!

CHAPTER 6

A PUZZLE

'It's shut!' whispered Brock. 'Shall I try and open it?'

'No!' said Pam.

'Yes!' said Peter. Pam clutched Peter's hand. She didn't know what she expected to find behind that closed door, but she felt certain it wouldn't be nice! The boys felt that they really *must* push the door open. They were bursting with curiosity. Brock pushed. It didn't open. He took hold of the iron handle and tried to turn it. It turned – but still the door didn't open.

'Look through the keyhole and see if you can see anything,' said Peter eagerly. 'It's so big that maybe you can.'

Brock put his eye to the keyhole. 'It's all so dark,' he said, 'but I believe I can make out shapes of boxes and things. You take a peep, Peter.'

So first Peter and then Pam peered through the keyhole, and they both agreed that certainly there were things there that hadn't been there before. They couldn't possibly see if they were boxes or trunks, or what they were, but there *were* things hidden there.

'If only we could get inside and see what's there!' said Brock longingly. 'Something that ought not to be there, I'm sure!'

The castle was so silent and lonely, and the sound of their whispering voices was so peculiar, echoing down the stone stairway, that Pam felt nervous again. She pulled at Peter's arm.

'Let's go,' she said. 'We'll come back another time. Shall we tell anyone about what we know?'

'I don't think so,' said Brock. 'It's our own mystery. We've discovered it. Let's try and solve it ourselves. We often read about secrets and mysteries in books – it would be fun to try and keep this one all to ourselves.'

They went downstairs again, puzzled to know what was in the tower, and why it was locked. When they got into the hall, Brock switched his torch towards the front door.

'I suppose the men came in at the front,' he began – and then, he suddenly stopped. 'Look!' he said. 'There are no footsteps leading from the front door. Isn't that strange? How did the men get in, then?'

The three children stared in silence at the enormous door. Certainly the men had not used it. Then which door had they used? As far as the children knew there was only one other door, and that was the little low one they themselves had used. They felt quite certain that the men had not used the window above, where the tree touched, because it was as much as the three children could do to squeeze inside there. No grown-up could possibly manage it.

'Let's follow all the footprints and see where they lead from,' said Brock. 'If we follow them all, we are sure to come to where the men entered.'

So, their torches directed on the ground, the children followed the tracks patiently, one after another. They couldn't understand one lot of tracks at all. They apparently led to, and came from, a room that had once been used as a study. The footprints went in and out of the door – there was a double-track, one going and one coming – and led across the room to the big fire-place, and back again.

'Why did the men come into this room, and out again?' said Pam, puzzled. 'They don't seem to have touched anything here. Why did they come here?'

'Goodness knows,' said Brock, switching off his torch. 'Just idle curiosity, or something, I suppose. There doesn't seem anything for them to come for, here. I say — look at the time. We shall be awfully late for tea!'

'We'd better go, then,' said Peter, who, although he wanted his tea, didn't want to leave the mystery unsolved like that. 'Come on. We'll come back again soon.'

They went into the kitchen and out of the little, low door. They pushed it to behind them, and piled the boughs against it, dragging the gorse bush round again. It hid the door well.

'I hope the men aren't as smart as we are!' said Brock, looking back at the castle. 'We've left plenty of footprints there for them to see. They could easily tell that three children have been wandering about.'

'I only wish I knew how the men got in and went out,' said Peter, still worrying about that. 'I feel sure there must be something in that room we last went into to account for their coming and going.'

But it wasn't until late that night, when Peter was in bed, that he suddenly thought of something most exciting! Why ever hadn't he thought of it before? He sat up in bed and called Brock's name in such an urgent voice that Brock, half-asleep, woke up in a hurry.

'What's up?' he said. 'More lights showing in Cliff Castle?'

'No,' said Peter. 'But I believe I know how the men got in and out, Brock!'

'You don't!' said Brock.

'Well, listen – you know that often there were secret ways made into and behind rooms through the big chimneys they had in the old days,' said Peter. 'Well, I believe there must be some kind of way into that room – and that's how the men got into the castle!'

'Crumbs!' said Brock, wide awake now. 'I never thought of that. I wonder if you're right. Maybe there's a secret entrance, then!'

'We'll jolly well go tomorrow and find out!' said Peter, 'even if we all get as black as sweeps exploring that chimney! What ho for a real adventure tomorrow!'

The two boys told Pam their idea in the morning, and the girl's eyes shone as she listened.

'Gracious! Do you really think there might be a secret way in and out of the castle through that big chimney-place? It's certainly enormous. I looked up it and it would take two or three men easily!'

To their disappointment the children could not go that day to the castle, because Brock's mother had planned a picnic for them. She was surprised when the three children did not seem pleased about it.

Next day the three children set off once more

to the castle. They knew the way very well now and took a few short cuts so that it did not take them very long to arrive at the bottom of the hill. They stared up at the great castle, and it seemed to look down on them with a frown.

'Frown all you like!' said Brock, with a grin. 'We'll find out your secret one day!'

They made their way to the little low door they knew and pulled it open. Into the vast kitchen they went, quite silently. Brock switched on his torch to see if there were any more footsteps to be seen. But there were none. In the hall and up the stairs were the same sets of prints that had been there before — there were no new ones, so far as the children could see.

'The men haven't been here again,' said Brock. 'Come on — let's go into that room where the prints led to and from the fireplace.'

So into it they went, and followed the sets of prints to the big, open chimney-place. This was of stone, and the three children could easily stand upright in it!

'Now, we'll just have a hunt and see if, by any chance, there's a way out of the chimney itself,' said Brock, and he switched his torch on to examine the stonework.

'Look!' cried Pam, pointing to something that ran up one side of the stone chimney. 'A little iron ladder!'

The three of them stared at the little ladder. In the middle of each rung the rust had been worn away a little. 'That's where the men went up and down!' cried Brock. 'Come on – up we go! We're on to something here!'

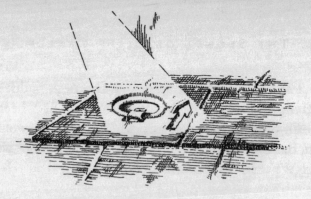

CHAPTER 7

A STRANGE PASSAGE

B rock went first up the little iron ladder.
Peter followed, and then Pam. The ladder
went up some way, and then ended.

'It's come to an end!' cried Brock. 'But there's
a broad ledge here. I'll give you a hand up,
Peter.'

He pulled Peter up on to the stone ledge, and
then the two boys pulled Pam up beside them.
The ledge was broad enough to hold all the children quite comfortably.

'This funny ledge seems to have been made
about half-way up the chimney, just before it
begins to get very narrow,' said Brock, pointing
his torch upwards, and showing the others how
the chimney suddenly narrowed just above their
heads. 'We couldn't have gone up much further,
even if there had been a ladder.'

'Well, what did the men do?' said Pam,

puzzled. 'Surely they didn't just come to this ledge and go back?'

'Of course not!' said Brock. 'This is where we use our brains a bit. Somewhere round about this ledge is the key to the secret passage that the men used. We've got to find it!'

'You don't mean a real key that turns, do you?' asked Pam, looking round and about with her torch, as if she expected to see a large iron key somewhere.

'Of course not,' said Brock impatiently. 'I don't exactly know what we're looking for, Pam – maybe a lever – or a handle of some sort – or a stone that moves when it's pushed. We just don't know till we try.'

So they tried. They hunted for any small bit of iron that might serve as a handle to move a stone. But they could find nothing in the walls around. They pushed against every stone they could reach, but they all seemed as solid as could be. They knocked with their knuckles to see if any stone sounded hollower than the rest, but except for taking the skin off their knuckles, there was no other result!

It was terribly disappointing. The children looked at one another, after about twenty minutes, and wondered what else to do.

'I'm afraid we're beaten,' said Peter, at last. 'There doesn't seem a thing here that might show us where a secret passage is.'

'There's only one place we haven't looked,' said Pam, suddenly.

The boys stared at her. 'We've looked simply everywhere!' said Brock. 'You know we have, silly.'

'Well, we haven't looked at the stones we're *standing* on!' said Pam. 'We've looked at the stonework around and above us – but not beneath our feet!'

'Pam's right!' said Brock excitedly. 'Good for you, Pam. You may be a girl, but you get the right ideas sometimes!'

Pam felt pleased. She only hoped she was right in her idea! The three of them knelt down to examine the stonework under their feet.

It wasn't long before Peter gave a loud cry, which made the others jump. 'Look! What's this in this stone?'

They all looked closely, shining their torches down. Set deep in a hole in the rough stone was a sunken iron handle. On the stone by the handle a rough arrow was carved, pointing towards the chimney hole.

'This is it!' cried Peter. 'Brock, what do we do? Pull at the handle?'

'Wait,' said Brock. 'This arrow means something. See where it points to? Well, I think we have to pull in that direction. Get off the stone, Pam, and Peter and I will see what we can do.'

Pam took her foot off the stone, and watched as the two boys took hold of the iron handle and heaved at it in the direction of the arrow. At first nothing happened at all – and then a very strange thing came to pass under their eyes!

As the boys heaved at the handle, the stone in which it was set began to move smoothly outwards as if it were on rollers! It moved towards the chimney hole, and then, when it seemed as if it really must overbalance and fall down the chimney, it stopped moving. In the space where it had been was a dark hole that led downwards!

'Look – there's something just a little way down, coiled up on a big staple!' cried Peter, and he shone his torch on it. 'It's a rope!'

Brock reached down and pulled it up. It wasn't a rope – it was a rope ladder. He saw that the top of it was firmly hitched to the staple, and the rest dropped down out of sight. He let go and the rope ladder swung back to its staple.

'Well, that's the way we go!' said Brock. He shone his torch on to Pam. 'What do you feel about it?' he asked. 'I know girls aren't so daring as boys. Would you like Peter to take you outside and leave you to wait in the sunshine somewhere, whilst we see where this goes to? It might be a bit dangerous.'

'Brock, don't be so mean!' cried Pam indignantly. 'I'm not a coward – and do you suppose I want to go away from here just when things are getting really thrilling? I'm coming with you, so that's that.'

'Righto,' said Brock, grinning. 'I thought you would. Don't get all hot and bothered about it. I'll go first. Peter, shine your torch down, old man.'

Peter shone his torch down the curious hole, and Brock let himself over the edge and felt about with his feet for the first rung of the rope ladder. Then down he went, very cautiously. After a bit, he shouted up: 'The ladder has come to an end. There's a stone floor here, and a passage leading off. Come on down. Send Pam first, Peter, then you can give her a hand down.'

So Pam went next, so thrilled that she could hardly feel for the rungs with her feet! She went down and down, and at last stood beside Brock, her feet safely on solid floor again. Then came Peter. They shone their torches into the passage that led off to the left of the strange hole.

'This is a real secret passage,' said Brock in an excited voice. 'A really proper one. Goodness — isn't it fun!'

'Come on,' said Peter. 'Let's see where it leads to. I can hardly hold my torch still, my hand is shaking so!'

They went down the narrow winding stone passage. It was perfectly dry, rather airless, and

very small. In places, the children had to bend their heads so as not to knock them against the roof of the passage.

The passage went steeply down, then at intervals turned right back on itself. 'It must be made in the walls of the castle itself,' said Brock wonderingly. 'What a funny thing for anyone to have thought of making. Hello – what's this?'

A shaft of daylight had suddenly appeared in one side of the passage! It came from an iron grille set in the wall of the passage itself.

'A sort of air-hole, I suppose,' said Peter, and he looked out. 'I say, do you know where we are? We are at the west side of the castle – the side that goes sheer down with the steep cliff. I believe there must be a way cut down through the cliff itself, and the entrance to it is somewhere at the bottom of it!'

'Yes – you're right,' said Brock, peering out too. 'Well, if that's so, the passage will soon change from a stone one to an earth one – and let's hope it hasn't fallen in anywhere.'

'Well, the men used it, didn't they?' said Peter.

Just as Brock said, the passage soon changed from a stone-walled one to one whose walls were made of earth, strengthened here and there by wood and stones. It zig-zagged down, and at the steepest places steps were cut. It was not an easy way to take.

'We must surely be nearly at the bottom!' said Brock, at last. 'My legs are getting jolly tired.'

There was still a little way to go – and then the secret passage ended abruptly in a small, low cave. The children crept into it, and then out into a larger cave. The entrance to this was set so closely about with gorse and blackberry bushes that it would have been quite impossible to see from the outside.

The children forced their way out, tearing their clothes and scratching their legs.

'You can see where the men got in and out,' said Brock. 'Just there, where sprays of bramble are broken.'

They looked round and about. They were now at the very bottom of the steep side of the cliff, where few people came. It was quite impossible to see the cave from where they stood, although they were only a few feet from it.

'Do you think we'd better climb back and swing that moving stone back into its place.' said Peter, suddenly. 'If the men come again, as it's pretty certain they will, they'll see that stone is moved, and suspect someone has been after them.'

Brock looked at his watch. 'We haven't time to do it,' he said in dismay. 'Gosh, Mother will be angry with us – it's half an hour past dinner-time already!'

'But, Brock – suppose the men see the stone is moved?' said Peter anxiously.

'We'll come back another time and put it into its place,' said Brock. 'Maybe the men won't be back for some time now. They don't come every night. Come on, now – we'll have to *race* back!'

And race back they did – but it didn't prevent them from being well scolded by Brock's mother!

CHAPTER 8
BROCK'S ADVENTURE

The children went to Brock's playhouse that afternoon, and talked and talked about their discoveries in the castle. They couldn't say enough about the finding of the strange secret passage. When they remembered that long dark climb downwards through the walls of the castle, and then down the cliff itself, they felt more and more thrilled.

But Peter also went on feeling uncomfortable about the stone in the chimney. He kept saying that the men might come back and discover it.

'Perhaps you're right,' said Brock, at last. "I'll slip off this evening, after tea, by myself, and put it back. It won't take me long now I know all the short cuts.'

'All right,' said Peter. But it was not to be, for Brock's mother wanted him to drive the pony-cart over to the farm and collect a crate of chickens for her.

'Oh, Mother! Won't it do tomorrow?' said Brock in dismay. 'I've got something I want to do this evening.'

'Well, I'm afraid *that* must keep till tomorrow,' said his mother. 'I've arranged with the farmer to send over for the chickens this evening and he'll have them all ready. Take Peter and Pam with you. It's a nice drive.'

So Brock had to go off with his cousins in the pony-cart. 'Just after I'd really made up my mind to go and do that at the castle,' he grumbled. 'I hate changing my plans. I really do feel you're right about that stone now, Peter.'

'So do I,' said Peter gloomily. 'It would be just our luck if the men came tonight!'

'I'll tell you what I'll do!' said Brock, suddenly. 'I'll go as soon as we're in bed! It will just be getting dark then, but the moon will be up early tonight, and I'll be able to see my way back beautifully.'

'Oooh, Brock! You surely don't want to go to the castle at night-time!' cried Pam in horror. She felt quite nervous enough in the daytime, and she knew she would never be brave enough to go at night!

'Why not?' said Brock with a laugh. 'You don't think I'm frightened, surely? It would take more than Cliff Castle to make *me* afraid!'

'Shall I come with you?' said Peter. He didn't really want to, but he felt he ought to make the offer.

'No, thanks,' said Brock. 'I think it would be best for just one of us to go.'

All Brock's family were early bedders, and it was about half-past ten when the boy got cautiously out of bed and began to dress himself. Twilight still hung about the fields, but would soon disappear. Then the moon would come up.

'Good luck, Brock!' whispered Peter. 'Do you think your father and mother are asleep?'

'I don't know,' said Brock. 'I'm not going to risk going downstairs and opening any of the doors. They are sure to creak!'

'Well, how are you going, then?' asked Peter, in astonishment.

'Down my old apple tree!' whispered Brock, and Peter saw the flash of his white teeth as he grinned.

He went to the window and put a leg across. He caught hold of a strong branch, and in a moment had worked his way down it to the trunk. Then down he slid and Peter heard the soft thud of his feet on the ground below. He watched the boy's shadowy figure as he ran down the garden and out into the lane. 'I hope he won't be too long,' thought Peter, as he curled up in bed again. 'I shall keep awake till he comes back. Then I'll pop up and wake Pam, and she can come down and hear what Brock has to say.'

But Peter didn't keep awake. By the time that half-past eleven had struck downstairs, he was fast asleep!

But Brock was wide awake, running like a hare over the fields. He met nobody, for no one was out so late at night in the country. Grazing sheep lifted their heads to look at him and a startled rabbit skipped out of his way.

Brock saw the moon coming up slowly. It lit up the castle on the hill, and made it look silvery and unreal.

'It's like a castle out of some old story,' thought the boy. 'It will be fun to get inside at night-time!'

Brock was quite fearless. He enjoyed this kind of adventure, and was quite glad to be on his own without the others to bother about. He ran round to where the little, low door was set at the bottom of the castle. He pulled at it and it opened.

He slipped inside. He waited a moment in the great dark kitchen to see if anyone else was about by any chance, but everything was still and silent. The boy switched his torch on, and went into the hall to see if there were any more footprints. But there were none. So the men hadn't yet been — but, after all, it wasn't many hours since Brock had left, and it didn't leave much time for anyone to come.

The boy made his way to the room where the iron ladder led up the chimney. He climbed up the ladder, and soon came to the ledge. The stone that had moved out to disclose the secret passage was still swung out over the chimney hole. Brock wondered how to get it back.

'I suppose I must heave on the iron handle in the opposite direction,' he thought. He took hold of it – and then almost fell down the hole in astonishment. He had heard voices!

'Gosh!' thought the boy, sitting quite still on the ledge, 'somebody is coming – two people at least. But where do the voices come from?'

Brock couldn't distinguish any words, he could only hear the murmur of voices, talking and answering. They came up from the hole, and were getting louder.

'My goodness, someone is coming up through the secret passage!' thought the boy, in a fright for the moment. 'It must be those men. I must get the stone back into place as quickly as I can!'

With the sound of voices came other sounds, rather like something being bumped against the wall. Brock felt sure the men were carrying something again. He took hold of the iron handle sunk in the stone and heaved hard at it. At first the stone would not move – then, slowly and gradually, it gave way to Brock's stout pulling, and rolled back into its place.

It made a slight grinding noise as it did so, and Brock hoped that the men below were talking loudly enough to drown the sound. He climbed quickly down the iron ladder and ran into the kitchen, meaning to get out of the little low door.

Then he stopped. 'No,' he said to himself. 'This is a big chance for me to find out exactly what the men are up to. I'll hide somewhere, and listen and follow. Goodness, what an adventure!'

He darted behind a big cupboard in the hall, and waited to see what happened. After some while he heard sounds coming from the room he had left. The men were climbing down the iron ladder in the chimney-place, dragging something heavy with them.

Then came the sound of voices, quite clearly echoing weirdly through the silent castle.

'We ought to be paid double for bringing the goods up that narrow way!' grumbled one voice. 'I'd be willing to risk the front door, but Galli won't hear of it. Come on – we've got to take the things up to the tower now. Then we'll get away quickly. I don't like this wretched moon, showing us up so clearly when we walk outside.'

From his hiding-place Brock could see two men, each carrying large and heavy boxes on their shoulders. They were half-bent beneath the weight, and the boy marvelled that they could possibly have carried them all the way up the secret passage, up the rope ladder, and then down the iron one!

'They must be very strong,' thought the boy. They were. They had broad shoulders, and when they were caught in a shaft of bright moonlight, Brock saw that they looked rather foreign. He had thought that their voices sounded a little foreign, too. One man wore gold earrings in his ears.

They came into the hall, carrying the boxes, and then went up the broad flight of stairs. They put the boxes down for a rest when they came to the top, and again Brock heard the murmur of their voices as they spoke together. The boy crept out from his hiding-place and went to the foot of the stairs.

He followed the men silently up and up until they went into the room from which the little stone staircase led into the tower room. One of the men unlocked the door at the top. Brock heard them put down their loads and sigh with relief.

'I could do with a drink now,' said one man. 'Is there a tap in the kitchen – or somewhere we can get water?'

'We'll look,' said the other. He locked the

door, and the men came down the narrow stair-case again. Brock saw that they had left the key in the door and his eyes gleamed. Maybe he could slip up and take it out before they remembered it – and then he and the others could come and find out what was in those boxes! Something exciting, he was sure!

He slipped out before the men, and ran into one of the nearby rooms. It was furnished, and the boy pulled some curtains around him to hide himself. But the things were quite rotten and fell away as he touched them. Thin grey dust flew all around, and before Brock could stop himself, he sneezed!

CHAPTER 9

BROCK IN TROUBLE

Now when Brock sneezed, everyone knew it, for he sneezed heartily and well. In the silence of the castle his sneeze made a most tremendous noise! It echoed all round and about, and startled poor Brock just as much as it startled the two men.

'There's someone here!' said one. 'In that room. Quick – we'll get him!'

They darted into the room where Brock had tried to hide. Luckily for him they missed him and he was able to dart out and elude their outstretched hands. He ran down the stairs at top speed, his boots making a tremendous clatter as he went.

The men ran after him. Down and down went Brock, meaning to make for the little low door in the kitchen. But when he got there, it was so dark he could not see where he was going and he fell over a stool. He crashed to the floor, and had no time to make for the door. Instead, he rolled quickly under a big oak seat in the fireplace and lay there, hardly daring to breathe. The men switched on their torches, and one of them gave an exclamation.

'Look here – here's a little door, ajar!'

'That's where the boy came in!' said the other man. 'Well, he didn't have time to get out, that's certain. He's somewhere here. But first I think we'll shut and lock the door. Then our friend won't be able to escape quite so easily as he hoped!'

Poor Brock heard the door being shut and locked. He felt certain that the man had put the key in his pocket. He couldn't think what to do. He wondered if the men knew of the little back staircase. If he could run up that he might be able to find the room where the big tree touched the window-sill. Then he'd be out in a jiffy and the men couldn't follow him!

'Let's shut the kitchen door, and have a good hunt round,' said one man. 'He's here somewhere.'

Now was Brock's chance. The big kitchen door was at the far end of the kitchen. He stood up quietly, and then made a dash for the little back staircase, which was quite nearby. The men gave a shout when they heard him, and switched their torches round to the noise.

'There's a stairway there!' cried one. 'He's gone up. Come on – after him!'

The men tore up the narrow stairway after Brock. 'If only I could remember which room that tree touched!' thought the boy desperately. 'But we couldn't find it again before. There are so many rooms here, all exactly the same!'

He ran on till he came to a room and then he darted inside. He took off his boots quickly because he knew that the noise they made gave him away and made him easy to follow.

The men passed the room, flashing their torches ahead of them. Brock ran to the window. Alas, it was not the right one. It was far too narrow to squeeze through.

Brock ran to the door and peered out. The men had gone to the other end of the stone landing and were looking into each of the rooms as they came back. Brock ran into the one next to his. Again he was disappointed. It was not the right one. He went into a third, his heart beating fast, for the men were now coming back. But again he was unlucky.

He did not dare to go into another room. The only thing he could do was to run back to the staircase and go down it, hoping to hide himself so well somewhere that he would not be found.

As he ran to the staircase the men saw him in a shaft of moonlight and raced after him. Brock almost fell down the stairs, and raced across the kitchen into the hall. Then he tore into one of the big, furnished rooms, meaning to hide behind some furniture.

The men saw him. They went into the room after him, and in a few moments they had found Brock and dragged him out from behind a big dusty couch that smelt so mouldy that the boy was almost sick.

'Well, we've got you now!' said the man. He shone his torch into Brock's face. 'What are you doing here, spying on us? You're doing a dangerous thing. We can't let you go, because you've found our secret, and we daren't risk your telling it till we've finished our job and are safe.'

Brock said nothing. His red, round face looked surly. The men looked at one another.

'What are we to do with him?' said one. 'He's only a kid. We'd better lock him up somewhere and tell Galli. Then he can put him away till it's safe to let him go. Well, youngster, you'll be sorry for yourself when Galli gets hold of you. He won't be gentle with a nasty little boy who spies on him!'

Still Brock said nothing. One of the men gave him a shake. 'He's lost his tongue,' he said to the other. 'Come on – let's lock him up in the tower room with the boxes. He'll be safe there.'

So Brock was dragged up to the tower room,

and put there among the big boxes. The men locked the door behind them, and Brock heard their footsteps going down the stairs. He felt sure they would go out by the little low door instead of the difficult way down the secret passage. And they would lock the door behind them, so that Peter and Pam couldn't get in if they came to look for him.

'I've made a mess of things,' said Brock, looking at the big boxes. 'I wonder what's in those boxes. How I'd like to know!'

He shone his torch on to one, but soon saw that it was so well fastened and nailed down that it would need strong tools to open it. His bare hands and pocketknife would be no good at all! He went to a window and looked out gloomily on the countryside. A ray of moonlight came through the slit. Far away, Brock could see his own house.

As he looked at it, he saw a light moving in one of the windows. He tried to reckon out which it was, and soon came to the conclusion that it was his own window. Then Peter must be awake. That must have been his torch shining!

In a trice Brock took out his own torch again, and pushed it as far as he could through the slit. He pressed the knob of the torch up and down, so that it flashed regularly and continually.

'If only Peter sees it, he may guess it's me,'

thought the boy. 'Oh, I do hope he sees it! I don't want to be kept a prisoner here for days!'

CHAPTER 10

PETER AND PAM
TO THE RESCUE!

Peter slept soundly till half-past one. Then he woke up with a jump. He remembered at once that Brock had gone to Cliff Castle, and he sat up in bed to see if the boy was back.

He stared at Brock's empty bed, and then switched on his torch to look at his watch. Half-past one! Whatever could Brock be doing?

As he sat wondering, he heard a sound at the door, and almost jumped out of his skin as a white figure came into the room. It was Pam in her nightdress.

'Peter! Is Brock back? You said you'd come up and wake me when he came back, but it's awfully late.'

Peter shone his torch on to Brock's empty bed. Pam felt scared.

'Goodness! Where is he?' She went to the window and stared out at the big black mass of Cliff

89

Castle. The moon had gone in for a moment, and it looked very dark and forbidding. Then she suddenly caught sight of a bright little light winking and blinking in the top tower to the right.

'That's funny,' she said to Peter. 'Look at that light, flashing every other moment, Peter, just as if it were a signal. Those men wouldn't do that, would they, because they wouldn't want to give themselves away. But who else would be signalling like that?'

Peter looked, and as soon as he saw the winking light he guessed that it was Brock. 'It's old Brock!' he said. 'I'm quite sure it is! What's he doing in the tower room – it was locked, wasn't it? He must have got in somehow and wants us to go and see what the treasure is in those boxes!'

'Or do you think he's been captured?' said Pam slowly. 'He might have been, you know. Maybe he's locked up in the tower.'

'We'd better go and see,' said Peter, beginning to dress hurriedly. 'We won't tell Aunt Hetty, or Uncle, Pam, in case Brock wants us to go and see the treasure with him without anyone knowing. We don't want to give the secret away unless we have to! Hurry and dress now!'

It wasn't long before the two children were climbing down the old apple tree and sliding to the ground below. Then they made their way to Cliff Castle, panting as they ran.

They got there safely, and went to where the little, low door was set in the kitchen wall. Peter pulled at it, expecting it to open. But it didn't. It remained tightly shut.

'I say! It's locked or something!' he said to Pam. 'Here, help me to pull.'

But pulling was no use at all. The little wooden door wouldn't budge!

'Well, Brock wouldn't have locked it, that's certain,' said Peter, speaking in a whisper. 'Someone else must have. I say – I rather think old Brock's been captured!'

'How shall we get in, then?' she whispered. 'Up that tree? But, Peter, surely we can't climb it in the dark.'

'We'll have to try,' said Peter. 'Look, the moon will be out for some time now – we'll climb whilst it gives us a bright light. I'll help you. Or would you rather stay on the ground whilst I climb?'

'No, I'll climb, too,' said Pam bravely. So they made their way to the tree and Peter shinned up it first. But Pam couldn't climb it because her legs trembled so. 'I'll just have to stay here,' she whispered up to him. 'I shall fall if I climb up, Peter. Isn't it sickening?'

'Never mind, old girl,' said Peter. 'You stay down below and warn me if anyone comes. I'll go in and see if I can rescue Brock.'

Pam couldn't see Peter climbing the tree because it was full of dark shadows, flecked by moonlight. She heard the rustling, though, and knew when Peter had reached the bough that led to the window because of the sudden swinging of the tree.

Peter didn't find it so easy to climb the tree in the dark as in the light, but he managed to slide down the branch to the window, and then squeezed himself through. He jumped down on the floor. His boots made a noise, and he took them off. He ran on tiptoe to the door, not making a sound. When he got there he looked out, and suddenly remembered how hard it had been to find that room again. He took one of his boots and made a big cross with it in the dust of the floor. Now he had only to pop his head in at the door to see the cross and know it was the room with the tree outside.

'I feel quite clever!' said the boy to himself. He ran to the little stone staircase and went lightly down it. The moon was now high and shone in at every slit-like window, so that it was fairly easy to see, though the shadows were as black as could be.

Across the kitchen went the boy, and into the dark hall. Then up the broad flight of stairs on the other side, and on to the first landing. He paused there in the shadows to listen. Was there anyone about? After all, if Brock had been captured, someone must have captured him – and it was quite likely they might still be somewhere in the castle. This was rather a weird thought, and the boy felt a shiver down his back.

'I won't get into a fright!' he thought to himself. 'I'm rescuing Brock, and I'm not afraid of anything.'

He would have liked to whistle to keep his spirits up, but he didn't dare to. As it was, every little sound he made went echoing round and round, and made him jump.

He went on up to the floor where the room was that had the tower staircase leading from it. He came to the stairway, and stood at the bottom, his heart beating so loudly that he felt sure anyone nearby could hear it!

He stole up the staircase, and felt the shut door. He longed to push it open, but he still didn't know if Brock was behind it, or an enemy. And then, suddenly, he knew!

There came the sound of a sigh, and then a creak as if someone had sat down on a box. 'Blow my torch!' said a gloomy voice. 'It's no use now – the battery's given out. I can't signal any more.'

It was Brock's voice. In delight Peter banged on the door, making poor Brock inside almost jump out of his skin, for he had, of course, no idea at all that Peter was anywhere near. He almost fell off the box.

'Brock!' came Peter's voice. 'I'm here. I'm coming. What's happened?' Peter pushed at the door – but alas, it was locked, and wouldn't open. Brock's voice came in excitement from behind the door: 'Peter! You old brick! Is the key in the lock?'

'No,' said Peter, switching on his torch. 'What a blow! I can't get in – and you can't get out.'

Brock told him shortly how he had been captured. 'And now I'm sitting on a box that may contain half the jewels in the kingdom!' he said. 'But I'm a prisoner, and likely to remain one till this man Galli they keep talking about comes along and decides what's to be done with me.'

'I'll go back home and get your father to come, and the police,' said Peter eagerly. 'I don't expect the men will be back tonight.'

'Where's Pam?' said Brock. 'Fast asleep in bed, I hope!'

'No. She's outside the castle, waiting,' said Peter. 'She couldn't climb the tree in the dark. She said she'd keep watch in case someone came.'

'I say, Peter! I've got an idea!' said Brock suddenly. 'Maybe the other towers have little rooms inside them, with a door like this one. And maybe they all have locks and keys that are the same. Do you think you could go to the tower on this side and see if there's a key in the door of the room there? If there is, bring it back and try it in this lock — it may fit — and open the door!'

'Gosh! That's an idea!' cried Peter, and he went down the staircase and made his way round the big stone landing until he came to the end. He went into the room there and found a staircase leading up to the tower above, exactly like the one in the room he had left. Up he went and came to a door.

'And, my goodness, there *is* a key in the lock!' said the boy to himself, in delight. He pulled out the key and made his way back. He fitted it into the lock of Brock's door — and it turned! The lock gave, and the door opened.

'Oh, Peter — what luck!' said Brock, and he squeezed his cousin's arm. 'Thanks, old man — you're a brick to rescue me. Now we must go straight down and join Pam — and then I think we ought to rush home and wake up my father. Someone ought to come and see what's in these boxes!'

Down the little stone staircase went the two boys, both in their socks. They felt tremendously excited, and Peter's hand shook as he held out his torch to show the way. The mystery of Cliff Castle was nearly solved. The secret was in those boxes. Soon Brock's father would come along and

open them. Then, maybe, the two men would be caught and everything would be cleared up.

Just as they reached the first landing they had a terrific shock. A great crashing echoed throughout the whole castle, and the two boys jumped so much that they had to stand still. What in the world could the noise be?

CHAPTER 11

MORE AND MORE EXCITEMENT

The enormous crash came again – and then the boys knew what it was!

'It's somebody banging on that great front door knocker!' cried Peter.

'But who would do that in the middle of the night?' said Brock, amazed.

'Pam, of course,' said Peter proudly. 'She said she'd watch out – and I expect she's seen someone coming and that's her way of warning us. What a marvellous idea!'

'I say – what a girl she is!' said Brock admiringly. 'Well – we'll have to look out. Let's slip down to the kitchen and see if we can get out of that little low door. Maybe the key is on this side.'

They ran quietly down the stairs in their socks – and then paused in horror. In the kitchen, waiting silently, themselves amazed at the noise from the front door, were three men. Two of them Brock had seen before.

The men saw the boys and gave a shout. 'Two kids this time!' cried one. 'Quick, get them!'

The boys tore into the hall and into the big room where the chimney was that gave on to the secret passage. Brock slammed the door and turned the key in the lock. Then they rushed to the fireplace and climbed quickly up the iron ladder. A heave at the iron ring and the stone moved silently across, showing the way down.

A great noise at the locked door made the boys hurry more than ever. The door would certainly be down very soon, for the lock was sure to be rotten!

It was! It gave way and the door swung open. The three men rushed in and paused. 'Surely those kids don't know the secret passage!' cried one of the men in amazement.

'They do!' said another. 'Come on – we must get them, somehow, or they'll be away, and tell the police.'

They rushed to the fireplace and swarmed up the iron ladder. By this time the boys were at the bottom of the rope ladder, making their way as quickly as they could down the secret stone passage, their hearts beating painfully.

They could hear the men coming after them, and hurried more and more. They came to where the stone passage ended and the earth passage began.

'Hurry, Brock, hurry!' cried Peter. 'They are almost on us. Hurry!'

Brock did hurry, but the ground was painful without his boots. At last the boys came to the small cave and made their way into the larger one. Just as the men got to the small cave the boys forced their way out of the large one, and found themselves on the hillside.

'Up a tree, quick!' whispered Brock. 'It's our only chance!'

Peter shinned up a nearby tree, with Brock helping him. Then Brock swung himself up into the dark shadows and both boys lay flat on branches, peering down below, hardly daring to breathe.

It didn't occur to the men that the boys could so quickly have gone up a tree. They thought they had run off into the bushes, and they beat about quickly to find them.

'They'll give it up soon,' whispered Brock. He was right. The men soon gave up the search and gathered together. The third man, called Galli, was very angry.

'Fancy letting a couple of kids beat you like this!' he said in disgust. 'Now there's only one thing to do – get the stuff out of the tower room at once and find a new hiding-place. Go on – get back to the castle and haul the stuff out.'

The men went off, the other two muttering angrily to themselves, but they were evidently terrified of Galli, who was the leader.

The men went back up the secret passage. As soon as they were safely out of hearing, the boys slid down the tree into the moonlight and looked at one another excitedly.

'Let's get back home as quickly as we can!' said Peter. 'We'll fetch Pam, and run as fast as possible.'

'The men will be gone by the time we get Dad and the police here,' panted Brock, as they ran up the slope that led to the front of the castle, to find Pam. She saw them coming and jumped out from under a bush.

'Brock! Peter! Oh, how glad I am to see you! Did you hear me crash on the knocker? I saw the three men coming, and they went in at that little low door. I couldn't *think* how to warn you – and I suddenly thought of that great knocker!'

'Pam, you're a marvellous girl!' said Brock, and he threw his arm round his cousin's shoulders and gave her a hug. 'Nobody but you would have thought of such an idea! Honestly, I'm proud of you!'

The boys quickly told Pam what had happened to them – and then Brock suddenly fell silent. The other two looked at him.

'What is it, Brock?' asked Peter.

'I've got an idea, but I don't know if it's good or not,' said Brock. 'Listen – those men are all going back to the tower room, aren't they? Well, do you suppose – do you *possibly* suppose we could get there, too, and wait till they're inside – and then lock them in?'

Peter and Pam stared at Brock. It seemed a mad idea – and yet – suppose, just suppose it could be done!

'The men would never, never guess we were back again,' said Peter slowly. 'They wouldn't be on the lookout for us. They think we're running off to tell the police. It seems to me that your idea is the only one that might possibly lead to the capture of the men – and the goods, too! Otherwise, by the time we get back here with help, they'll be gone with everything!'

'We'll try it!' said Brock. 'Now, look here, Pam – your part in this is to race off by yourself over the fields and wake Daddy and Mother, and tell them everything. Will you do that?'

Pam didn't at all want to do anything of the sort, but she wasn't going to let the boys down. She nodded her head. 'I'll go,' she said, and she went, running like a little black shadow down the hillside.

'She's a good kid,' said Brock, and the two boys turned to go to the castle. They meant to climb up the tree and get in that way. They were sure the little low door would be locked. Up they went and into the dark room. There, on the floor, was the cross in the dust that Peter had made!

'Now quietly!' whispered Brock, as they went down the narrow stone staircase. 'The men may be in the kitchen, or the hall.'

The boys stole carefully down. There was no one in the kitchen – and no one in the hall. The boys kept to the shadows as they walked.

Suddenly they heard a noise, and Peter clutched Brock by the arm, pulling him into the shadow of a great hall curtain. 'It's the men coming out of the chimney-place,' whispered the boy. 'They're only just back. It's taken them ages to come up by that steep secret passage. Keep quiet now. We may be able to do something.'

The men clattered across the room to the door and then went across the hall to the big staircase, talking in loud voices. It was quite clear that they had no idea at all that the boys were hidden nearby. They went up the stairs, and as soon as they had turned a corner, the boys followed them, so full of excitement that they could hardly breathe!

The three men went on up to the tower room. The boys could hear their voices all the time.

They crept after them in their socks. They had never felt so terribly excited in their lives!

All the men went into the tower room. Peter and Brock stood at the bottom of the little staircase that wound up to the room, and wondered if this was the right moment to go up.

'Better do it now,' said Brock, 'or they will start to come out again.'

Galli, up above, gave orders to the two men. 'Take that box first. And hurry up about it!'

There came the sounds of two men swinging a box round to get hold of it.

'Now!' whispered Brock, and the two boys shot up the stairs, one behind the other, breathing fast. They got to the door. The men hadn't heard a sound. By the light of their torches Brock could see two of them lifting one of the boxes, whilst Galli stood by. The boy caught hold of the wooden door, and closed it as quietly as he could. But it made a slight click as the latch went into place. At once Galli noticed it and roared out a warning.

'Look out! There's somebody on the stairs!' he rushed to the door. But Brock had already turned the key in the lock.

Galli hammered on the door in a rage and the stout door shook under his blows.

'Hammer all you like!' shouted Brock exultingly. 'You're caught!'

The boys turned to go down the stairs – and then Peter's sharp ears caught something that one of the men said.

'I've got a key to this door! I took it out of the lock when I shut up that kid. Here, take it, Galli, and undo the door. We'll catch those boys if we have to hunt the castle from top to bottom!'

Peter clutched Brock by the arm. 'Did you hear that? They've got the key to this door, Brock! The one that was in the door when they locked you up! Now what are we to do?'

Brock dashed up the stairs again. He switched his torch on to the door, at the same moment as he heard a key being put into the lock from the other side. His torch showed him a big bolt at the top of the door and another at the bottom. Hoping and praying that they would not be too rusty to push into place, the boy took hold of the bottom bolt. He pulled at it, but it stuck badly.

Meantime the men on the other side of the door were trying to turn the key to unlock it. But it was more difficult to do that from inside than outside. Muttering a string of foreign-sounding words, Galli tried to force the key round.

'Let me try the bolt, Brock,' whispered Peter, and took Brock's place. But it was no use. He could only move it a little way, it was so rusty.

'Try the top one,' said Brock. So Peter stood

on tiptoe and tried the one at the top. He was trembling from head to foot, for it was terrible to hear someone doing his best to unlock the door from the inside, whilst he, Peter, was trying with all his might to bolt it from the outside!

'Oh Peter, Peter, won't it move?' groaned Brock, feeling certain that they would be captured if the door was unlocked. Peter suddenly gave a shout, and there was a creaking sound. The rust on the bolt had given way and the bold had slid slowly into place. The door was bolted!

Almost at the same moment the key turned on the other side and unlocked the door – but it was held by the bolt, and Galli roared with rage as he found that the door would not budge. It gave at the bottom, but the stout bolt at the top held firmly.

The boys were both shaking. They had to sit down on the stairs and lean against one another. Neither boy could have gone down the stairs at that moment. They sat there, close to each other, and heard the three men losing their tempers with one another. They shouted in a strange language, and at times one of them would shake the door with all his strength.

'I hope that top bolt holds,' said Peter in a whisper. 'Everything in this house is so rotten and old that I wouldn't be surprised if the wretched thing gives way.'

'Well, let's try to use the bottom bolt as well then, when the men leave the door alone for a moment,' whispered back Brock. 'Come on – there's a chance now.'

The boys, both together, tried to move the bottom bolt back into place. Peter took Brock's knife and scraped away the rust as best he could. Then they tried again – and to their great joy and relief, the bolt slowly and haltingly slipped into place. Now the door was held at top and bottom, and the boys felt pretty certain that the men could not possibly get out, even if they tried all their strength together on the door.

The men did try once more – and this time they found, of course, that it would not move at the bottom.

'They've fastened the door at the bottom, too, now!' shouted Galli, and the angry man struck the door with his fists, and kicked at it viciously with his foot.

'Hope he hurts himself!' whispered Brock, who was feeling much better now. He had stopped shaking, and was grinning to himself to think how neatly all the men were boxed up together. 'I say, Peter – I rather think we've done a good night's work!'

'I rather think we have, too!' said Peter, and the two boys hugged themselves as they thought of all they had gone through to catch the men.

'I hope Pam gets home safely,' said Brock. 'I wonder how long it will be before she brings help back. Some time, I expect, because Dad will have to get in touch with the police. Well – I'm quite content to wait here till somebody arrives. I guess we're feeling a bit more comfortable than those three men!'

CHAPTER 12

THE SECRET COMES OUT!

Meantime Pam was speeding across the fields and along the shadowy lanes. Once she had started she no longer felt afraid. She had to bring help to the boys, and that help rested on her swift feet. 'Quick, quick!' she kept saying. 'I must run like the wind!'

And run like the wind she did. She came to her aunt's house at last, and hammered on the front door, for she did not want to waste time by climbing in at the window. Her uncle awoke at once and came to his window. When he saw Pam standing there in the moonlight he thought he must be dreaming.

'Uncle! Uncle! Let me in, quick!' cried Pam. 'There isn't a moment to be lost! The boys are in danger!'

In two minutes Pam was inside the house, sitting on her uncle's knee, pouring out the whole story to him as quickly as she could. He and his wife listened in the utmost amazement. Aunt Hetty could hardly believe the story, but Pam's uncle did at once, and saw that he must act quickly.

'I'll hear all the rest later,' he said to the excited little girl. 'If those two boys have managed to capture the men as they planned, we must go there at once – and if they haven't managed to, they'll be in the gravest danger. I'll ring up the police now. Hetty, see to Pam. She'd better go back to bed.'

But nothing in the world would have persuaded Pam to go back to bed that night! 'I'll climb out of the window if you make me go to bed!' she cried. 'Oh, Aunt Hetty, I *must* go back to Cliff Castle. I must, I must!'

And, as it turned out, she did, because when her uncle came back from the telephone he said that the police wanted her to go with them to take them to the right room. It wasn't long before a police car roared up to the house with four stout policemen inside!

Pam and her uncle squeezed into the car too, and they set off to Cliff Castle by the road. It was a much longer way than across the fields, but it didn't take very long in the powerful police car.

'Why, look at that light in the sky!' said Pam

suddenly, pointing to the east. 'What is it, Uncle?'

'It's the dawn coming!' said her uncle, with a laugh. 'The night is going. Hasn't it been a long enough night for you, Pam?'

'Yes, it has,' said Pam, suddenly feeling glad that the daylight would soon be there. 'I wonder how we can get into the castle, Uncle? There are four ways in – but three of them are almost impossible.'

'What are the four ways, Missy?' asked the inspector, who was sitting beside her.

'There's the front door,' said Pam, 'but the locks and bolts are all rusted, and we couldn't open it. Then there's a little, low door set in the foot of the castle by the kitchen – but that's shut and locked. And there's a secret passage from the bottom of the steep cliff, through the walls of the castle, and up a chimney.'

'My word!' said the inspector, startled. 'However did you find out all this? I must say you children are pretty daring! What's the fourth way in?'

'It's the way we used first,' said Pam. 'Up a tree and in at a window. But I'm afraid you're all too big to squeeze in there!'

'We'll break in at the little, low door!' said the inspector with a chuckle. And that is exactly what they did do!

The two boys were still sitting together on the stairs, feeling rather sleepy, watching the dawn put silver fingers in at the slits of window, when they suddenly heard the noise of the police car roaring up to the castle. Then they heard loud blows on the little door far below.

'They're breaking in!' cried Brock, in excitement, and he jumped to his feet, almost falling down the stairway. 'They're knocking down that little door. Now they're in – gosh, they're here! Pam! Pam! Here we are!'

Pam came tearing up the big staircase, followed by her uncle and the four policemen. She rushed into the room off which the little winding stairway led up to the tower room, shouting as she came.

'Peter! Brock! Did you manage to catch the men? Uncle's here and four policemen!'

'Yes, we've got the men!' shouted Brock, and grinned as he saw Pam's excited face coming round the bend in the stairway. 'We've bolted them in well and truly!'

The men had fallen silent when they heard the shouts. They knew perfectly well that everything was up, as far as they were concerned.

'Get away down the stairs, you three children,' commanded the inspector, suddenly taking on a new and quite stern voice. The children badly wanted to be in at the finish – but they didn't dare to say a word. They had to go and wait in the room below whilst the police unbolted the door and rushed the three men.

There was a lot of yelling and struggling, but the five men against the three were too strong, and it wasn't long before a sorry procession came down the winding stairway in the charge of three policemen.

'Take them into a room and stay with them till I come,' ordered the inspector. Then he beckoned to the three children.

'Come along,' he said, 'we're going to open those boxes. You deserve to see what's inside, since it was you who really captured the men!'

In the greatest excitement, the children followed the inspector and Brock's father upstairs into the tower room. The great boxes lay there, still unopened.

The inspector had the right tools with him and began to force open the boxes quickly. They were very well fastened indeed, and even when the clasps had been forced back, the ropes cut, and the iron bands severed, there were still the locks to open. But the inspector had marvellous keys for these. 'One of these keys will open the locks,' he told the watching children. 'It's my boast that I've got keys to open any lock in the world!'

The locks of the first box clicked. The inspec-

tor threw back the heavy lid. What looked like
cotton wool lay on the top. Pam pulled it aside.
Then everyone cried out in astonishment and
awe – for lying in the box were the most marvellous jewels that the children had ever seen or
heard of. Great red rubies shone and glowed in
necklaces and tiaras. Brilliant green emeralds
winked, and diamonds blazed in the light of the
torches that shone down on the jewels.

'I say!' said Brock's father, finding his tongue
first. 'I say – inspector, these are not ordinary
jewels. They are worth a fortune – many for-
tunes! What are they?'

'Well, it looks to me as if they are the private
jewellery of the Princess of Larreeanah,' said the
inspector. 'They were stolen on the ship, when
she fled from her palace in India to this country.
It's an amazing story. She had them all put into
these boxes and safely fastened in many ways.
They were put into the stronghold of the ship
she took. They were apparently guarded night
and day – and were taken ashore with her when
she landed in this country. But when the boxes
were opened at her bank in London, they contained nothing but stones!'

'But how could that be?' said Pam, her eyes
opening wide in amazement. 'And how are they
here, then?'

'Well, I suppose what happened was that one

of the guards on the ship was bribed by some clever thief who knew what was contained in the boxes,' said the inspector. 'He must have had boxes of exactly the same size and make all ready, filled with stones – probably hidden inside big trunks of his own. At the right moment he must have got into the place where these boxes were stored, exchanged them, and then put these boxes into his own big trunks, and gone ashore safely with them.'

'And the poor princess went off with the boxes of stones!' cried Brock. 'Was it that man Galli, do you think?'

'Yes, I should think so,' said the inspector, beginning to open another box. 'He's very like a famous thief, one of the cleverest we have ever come up against, whom we already want for another daring robbery. He's shaved off his moustache and beard, but I noticed that he had a little finger missing – and so has this thief I was telling you about! My word – look at this!'

The second box was now open, and contained just as amazing treasures as the first. Pam took out a wonderful tiara, rather like a small crown, and put it on.

'Now you're worth about fifty thousand pounds!' said her uncle. 'Do you feel grand and important?'

'Oh, very!' said Pam, with a laugh.

'Well, you've every right to feel like that,' said the inspector, shutting the first box and locking it. 'But not because you're wearing famous jewels. You can feel grand and important because you and your brother and cousin have made it possible for us to recover all this jewellery and to catch the thieves who stole it! At the moment I should say you are the most daring and clever children in the whole country!'

Even Brock blushed at this. All the children felt pleased.

'Well, it didn't seem very clever or daring whilst we were doing it,' said Peter honestly. 'As a matter of fact, I kept feeling frightened – and I know poor old Pam did.'

'It's braver to do a thing if you feel afraid than it is to do it if you don't mind,' said the inspector. 'I don't know what to do with these boxes. I think I'll handcuff those three men together, send them off in charge of two of my men, and leave the third man here on guard whilst I go and report to Scotland Yard.'

'What's Scotland Yard?' said Pam in surprise.

'It's the place where all the head policemen work!' said the inspector, with a sudden grin. 'Very important place, too! Well – come along. You children must be tired out.'

They went down the stairs. The inspector gave his orders, and the three sullen thieves were handcuffed together, so that two policemen could easily take charge of them. The third one was sent up to guard the tower room.

'I'll send back a car for Galli and the others,' said the inspector. 'I'll take these children home, and then their uncle can come along with me to the station.'

Pam almost fell asleep in the car. She was completely tired out. But the two boys were still excited. They looked out of the car windows at the sun just rising in the eastern sky. It seemed ages and ages since yesterday! Could so much have possibly happened in one night?

Brock's mother made all the children go to bed when they got back. 'You look absolutely worn out,' she said. 'Tell me everything when you wake, Pam. I'll undress you. You are falling asleep as you stand!'

The boys were glad to get into bed now, though it seemed odd to go to bed when the sun was just rising. Brock snuggled down.

'Well, good night,' he said to Peter. 'I mean, good morning! What adventures we've had. I'm sorry they're over. I did enjoy solving the mystery of Cliff Castle.'

'Yes, we soon found out the secret,' said Peter. 'But, oh – I'm sorry it's all ended!'

But it hadn't quite ended. The Princess of Larreeanah was so overjoyed at the recovery of her jewels that she came herself to see the three adventurous children.

She arrived in a magnificent car, and was wearing some of the jewels. Much to the children's embarrassment, she kissed them all.

They didn't like being kissed by strangers, even if this stranger was a princess – and they made up their minds they weren't going to like her. But they soon changed that idea when they found what she had brought for them in a small van that followed her car!

'Open the door of the van and see what is inside for you!' she said to the three surprised children. Brock pulled open the doors at the back of the van – and all three stared in amazement and awe at the Princess's wonderful present.

'It's a car – a small car just big enough to take the three of us!' said Brock, staring at the marvellous little car inside the van. It was bright red, with yellow bands and yellow spokes to the wheels. The lights, wind screen and handles shone like silver.

'It goes by electricity,' said the princess. 'I had it made especially for you. You don't have to have a driving licence, of course, because it is listed as a toy car. But actually it is driven just like a real one, has a horn and everything, and goes by electricity, so that you don't need petrol.'

'Let's go for a ride in it now!' shouted Peter in excitement. So they pulled out the magnificent little car and got into it. Brock drove it. He pulled a lever, took hold of the steering wheel, and off went the car down the lane with its three excited passengers.

'What a wonderful end to an adventure!' cried Peter. 'Didn't I say we'd have real, proper adventures? And wasn't I right?'

Well – he certainly was!

The Children of
Kidillin

The Children of
Kidillin

Enid Blyton
Illustrations by Patricia Ludlow

BLOOMSBURY
CHILDREN'S
BOOKS

Contents

CHAPTER 1

THE MEETING OF THE FOUR COUSINS

Two children and a dog raced down to the village sweet-shop in excitement. They opened the little door of Mrs MacPherson's shop and went inside.

'Good morning,' said Mrs MacPherson, in her soft Scottish voice. 'You looked excited, the two of you.'

'We are,' said Sandy, a tall boy with a jolly, freckled face. 'We've got our English cousins coming to live with us till the war's over! We've never even seen them!'

'They're about the same age as we are,' said Jeanie, Sandy's sister. 'One's called Tom, and the other's called Sheila. They live in London, but their parents want them to go somewhere safe till the war's over. They're coming tomorrow!'

'So we've come down to get some of your bull's-eye peppermints for them,' said Sandy.

'And will they do lessons with Miss Mitchell your governess?' asked Mrs MacPherson, getting down her big jar of peppermint humbugs. 'It will be right nice company for you.'

'It's to be hoped the town children don't find it dull down here,' said Mrs MacPherson, handing over a fat bag of sweets. Sandy and Jeanie stared at her in surprise.

'*Dull!*' said Jeanie, quite crossly. 'How could anyone find Kidillin dull? There's the river that rushes through Kidillin, and the hills around, and away yonder the sea!'

'Ay, but there's no cinema for twelve miles, and only three shops, not a train for ten miles, and no buses!' said Mrs MacPherson. 'And what will town children do without those, I should like to know?'

The two children left the little shop. They gazed into the two other ships of Kidillin – which were general stores, and sold most things – and then made their way home again, each sucking a peppermint.

Sandy and Jeanie were really indignant at the thought that anyone could be bored with Kidillin. They loved their quiet Scottish life, they loved Kidillin House, their home, and enjoyed their lessons with Miss Mitchell, their old governess. They knew every inch of the hills about their home, they knew the flowers that grew there, the birds and the animals that lived there, and every cottager within miles.

Sandy and Jeanie were to drive to the nearest town to meet their cousins the next day. So, with Miss Mitchell driving the horse, they set off. It was a long way, but the autumn day was bright and sunny, and the mountains that rose up around were beautiful. The children sang as they went, and the clip-clop of the horse's feet was a pleasant sound to hear.

The train came in as they arrived at the station. Sandy and Jeanie almost fell out of the trap as they heard its whistle. They rushed through the little gate and on to the platform.

And there stood a boy and girl, with a pile of luggage around them – and a dog on a lead!

'Hello!' cried Sandy. 'Are you Tom and Sheila?'

'Yes,' said the boy. 'I suppose you are Sandy and Jeanie? This is our dog, Paddy. We hope you don't mind us bringing him – but we couldn't, we really *couldn't* leave him behind!'

'Well, I hope he gets on all right with *our* dog,' said Sandy doubtfully. 'Mack is rather a jealous sort of dog. Come on. We've got the trap outside. The porter will bring out your luggage.'

The four children, the dog, and a porter, went out to Miss Mitchell. She shook hands with Tom and Sheila, thought that Sheila was very pretty,

but far too pale, and that Tom was too tall for his age. But they had nice manners, and she liked the look of them.

'Welcome to Scotland, my new pupils!' said Miss Mitchell. 'Get in – dear me, is that your dog? I hope he won't fight Mack.'

It looked very much as if Paddy would certainly fight Mack! The two dogs growled, bared their teeth and strained hard at their leads. Their hair rose on their necks and they looked most ferocious.

'What an unfriendly dog Mack is,' said Tom. This was not at all the right thing to say. Sandy looked angry.

'You mean, what an unfriendly dog your Paddy is,' he said. 'Our Mack would have been pleased enough to see him if he hadn't growled like that.'

'Mack can come up on the front seat with me,' said Miss Mitchell hastily. She didn't want the cousins to quarrel within the first five minutes of their meeting.

'Then I shall drive,' said Sandy at once. He wasn't going to sit behind in the trap and talk politely to a boy who was rude about Mack.

'Can you drive this trap yourself?' said Sheila in surprise.

'Of course,' said Sandy. 'I've driven it since I was four.' He thought Sheila was rather a nice girl – but Jeanie didn't! Jeanie thought Sheila was too dressed-up for anything!

'How does she think she's going to walk on the hills in *those* shoes?' thought Jeanie scornfully, looking at Sheila's pretty button-shoes. 'And what a fussy dress! All frills and ribbons! But I like Tom. He's nice and tall.'

They drove home. Miss Mitchell did most of the talking, and asked the two London children all about the home they had left. They answered politely, looking round at the countryside all the time.

'Doesn't it all look awfully big, Sheila,' said Tom. 'Look at those mountains! Oh – what a funny little village! What is it called?'

'It is Kidillin,' said Jeanie. 'We live not far away, at Kidillin House. Look – you can see it above those trees there.'

Sheila and Tom looked at the plain, rather ugly stone house set on the hillside. They did not like the look of it at all. When they had gone to stay with their uncle in the English country-side the year before, they had lived in a lovely old thatched cottage, cosy and friendly – but this old stone house looked so cold and stern.

'I hope the war will soon be over!' said Tom, who really meant that he hoped he wouldn't have to stay very long at Kidillin. Sandy and Jeanie knew quite well what he was really thinking, and they were hurt and angry.

'They are as unfriendly as their dog!' whispered Jeanie to Sandy, as they jumped down from the cart. 'I'm not going to like them a bit.'

'I wish we were at home!' whispered Sheila to Tom, as they went up the steps to the front door. 'It's going to be horrid, being here!'

CHAPTER 2

THE OLD COTTAGE ON THE HILLSIDE

For the first few days things were very difficult for all four children, and for the two dogs as well. They were even more difficult for poor Miss Mitchell! Sandy and Jeanie never quarrelled – but now she had four children who bickered and squabbled all day long!

As for the dogs, they had to be kept well apart, for they each seemed to wish to tear the other to pieces! They had to take it in turns to be tied up so that they could not fly at one another all day long.

'And really, I'm wishing I could tie up the children too,' Miss Mitchell said to Sandy's mother. 'For they're like the dogs – just ready to fly at one another's throats all day long!'

Mrs MacLaren laughed. 'Give them time to settle down to each other,' she said. 'And you'd better begin lessons again tomorrow, Miss

Mitchell – that will keep them out of mischief a bit.'

Sandy and Jeanie had been showing off to Tom and Sheila. They had taken them for a long walk, up a difficult mountain, where a good deal of rough climbing had to be done. The English children had panted and puffed, and poor Sheila's shoes were no use at all for such walking.

'Can't we have a rest again?' asked Sheila at last. 'I'm so tired. This is a dreadful place for walking. I'd much rather walk in the park!'

'In the *park*!' said Sandy scornfully. 'What, when there's fine country like this, and soft heather to your feet! And look at the view there – you can see the sea!'

The four children sat down. Far away they could see the blue glimmer of the sea, and could hear very faintly the shrill cry of the circling gulls. Tom was so tired that he only gave the view a moment's look, and then lay down on his back. 'Phew, I'm tired!' he said. 'I vote we go back.'

'But we're not yet at the burn we want to show you,' said Jeanie. Sheila giggled.

'It does sound so funny for a stream to be called a *burn*!' she said. 'It sounds as if something was on fire – going to see the *burn*!'

'The bur-r-r-rn, not the *burn*,' said Sandy, sounding the *R* in burn. 'Can't you talk properly?'

'We can talk just as well as *you*!' said Tom, vexed, and then off they went, squabbling again!

Mack, who was with the children, barked when he heard them quarrelling. He wanted someone to quarrel with too! But Paddy was at home, tied up, much to Tom's annoyance.

'Be quiet,' said Tom to Mack. 'I can't hear myself speak when you begin that noise. Where are you going, Sandy? I want to rest a bit more.'

'There'll be no time to finish the walk if you lie there any longer,' said Sandy. 'This is the fourth time we've stopped for you – a lazy lot of folk you Londoners must be!'

'All right. Then we'll *be* lazy!' said Tom angrily. 'You and Jeanie go on, and Sheila and I will stay here till you come back – and you can go and find your wonderful bur-r-r-r-rn yourself!'

'Oh do come, Tom,' begged Jeanie. 'It really is a strange sight to see. The water comes pouring out a hole in the hillside – just as if somebody had turned a tap on!'

'Well, don't you go rushing up the mountain so quickly then,' said Tom, getting up. 'I'm sure you're just showing off! I bet you and Jeanie don't go so fast when you're alone! You're just trying to make us feel silly.'

Jeanie went red. It was quite true – she and Sandy had planned together to take the two Londoners for a stiff walk up the mountains, going at a fast pace, just to show them what Scots children could do. And now Tom had guessed what she and Sandy had planned.

'Oh come on,' said Sandy impatiently. They all went up the steep, heathery slope, rounded a big crag, and then slipped and slid on a stony stretch that scratched Sheila's shoes to bits!

Suddenly there was a rumble of thunder round the mountain. Tom looked up anxiously. 'I say! Is there going to be a storm?' he said. 'Sheila always gets a cold if she gets soaked. Is there anywhere to shelter?'

'There's an old tumble-down hut not far from here,' said Sandy. 'Come on – run!'

The rain began to fall. The four children and the dog ran full-pelt over the heather – up another slope, round a group of wind-blown pine trees – and there, in front of them, tucked into the mountainside, was an old, tumble-down cottage!

The children rushed to the door, flung it open and ran inside. They shook themselves like dogs, and the rain flew off their clothes, just as it was flying off Mack's coat. Then Sandy gave a cry of surprise.

'I say! Somebody lives here! Look!'

The children looked around the little stone house. It was roughly furnished with chairs, a table and two camp beds. An oil-stove stood in a corner, and something was cooking on it.

'Funny!' said Jeanie, staring round. 'Nobody's here at all – and yet there's something cooking on the stove.'

'Perhaps there's someone in the tiny room at the back,' said Sandy, and he pushed open the door and looked inside. The boy stopped in the greatest surprise. Nobody was there – nobody at all – but the whole room seemed full of a strange-looking machine, that had knobs and handles, valves and levers on it. Sandy was just going to tell Tom to come and see, when he heard footsteps.

He shut the door of the little room quickly, just as the door of the house swung open, and a fat man came in. He was so astonished when he saw the children that he couldn't say a word. He stood and gaped at them in amazement. Then he turned a purple-red and caught Tom by the shoulder.

He made peculiar noises, and pushed the boy out of the door so roughly that he almost fell. He was just about to do the same to Jeanie when Sandy stepped up and stopped him. The boy stood there in his kilt, glowering at the angry man.

'Don't you dare touch my sister!' he said. 'What's up with you? There was a storm coming on, and we came in here out of the rain. We didn't know anyone lived here – it's always been empty before. We'll go if you don't want to give us shelter!'

There was the sound of footsteps again and another man came into the house, looking dismayed and astonished. He began to roar at the children.

'What are you doing here? Clear out! If you come here again I'll set my dog on you!'

The children stumbled out of the old hut in a fright. The second man caught hold of Tom and shook him. 'Did you go into the room at the back?' he demanded. 'Did you? Go on, answer me! If you've come to steal anything, you'll be sorry.'

'Of course we haven't come to steal anything!' said Tom indignantly. 'No, I didn't go into any room at all except the one you found us in — I didn't even know there *was* another room! So keep your silly secrets to yourself!'

The man made as if he would rush at him, but Mack somehow got in between, and tripped the man over. He sat up nursing his ankle, looking as black as thunder.

'Loose the dog, Carl!' he yelled. 'Loose the dog.'

'Come on,' said Sandy at once. 'It's a big brute of a dog. I can see it over there. It would eat Mack up!'

The four children flew down the path in the

rain. No dog came after them. The rain poured down, and Tom looked anxiously at Sheila again. 'We really shall have to shelter somewhere,' he said. 'Sheila is getting soaked and I promised Mother I'd look after her.'

'There's an overhanging rock by the burn we wanted to show you,' said Sandy stopping. 'But it's rather near that old hut. Still, the men won't see us there, and they'll think we've gone home frightened, anyway. Come on!'

Sandy led the way. In a few minutes they came within the sound of rushing water, and then Tom saw a great craggy rock. They went towards it, and were soon crouching under it out of the rain.

'This is the burn, or stream we wanted to show you,' said Sandy. 'Look – it gushes out of the hole in this rock – isn't it strange? It comes from the heart of the mountain – we always think it's very strange.'

It *was* strange. There was a large, uneven hole in one side of the great rock, and from it poured a clear stream of water that fell down the mountainside in a little gully it had made for itself. On and on it went down the mountain until, near the bottom, it joined the rushing River Spelter.

'Jeanie and I have climbed down beside this water all the way from this stone to the river,' said Sandy proudly. 'It's very difficult to do that. We had to take a rope with us to get down at some places, because the burn becomes a water-fall at times!'

Tom was very interested in the torrent that poured out of the hole in the rock. He went close up to it and peered into the hole, whose mouth was almost hidden by the spate of water.

'Does this water get less when there are no rains?' he asked. Sandy nodded. 'Yes,' he said, 'it's very full now, for we've had heavy rains the last week or two. Wouldn't it be exciting to crawl through that hole, when the water was less, and see where it led to!'

'Where does the River Spelter rise?' asked Tom. 'In this same mountain?'

'Nobody knows,' said Sandy. Tom looked astonished.

'But hasn't anyone followed it up to see?' he asked.

'No,' said Sandy with a laugh. 'It's like this burn here – it suddenly flows out of the mountain, and no one has ever dared to seek its source, for it would mean swimming against a strong current, in pitch black darkness, underwater! And who would care to do that!'

'How peculiar,' said Tom thoughtfully. 'This is a more exciting place than I thought – springs that gush out of rocks, and rivers that come from underground homes – and strange men that live in secret tumble-down huts!'

'Let's start home again now,' said Sandy, suddenly remembering the two men and their dog. 'It's stopped raining. Tom, remind me to tell you something when we get back.'

Down the mountain they went – and poor Sheila quickly decided that it was far worse to go down steep slopes than to go *up* them! She was tired out when at last they reached Kidillin House.

'Oh, Sandy, you shouldn't have taken Tom and Sheila so far,' said Miss Mitchell, when she saw Sheila's white, tired face. 'And look – the child's soaked through!'

Sandy and Jeanie were ashamed of themselves when they saw that Sheila really was too tired even to eat. They went to tie up Mack, and to let Paddy loose.

'Anyway, we've shown Tom and Sheila what sillies they are when it comes to walking and climbing!' said Sandy. 'Oh – where's Tom? I wanted to tell him something!'

He found Tom groaning as he took off his boots. 'My poor feet!' he said. 'You're a wretch, Sandy – you wait till I find something I can do better than you!'

'Tom,' said Sandy. 'Listen. I peeped inside the back room of that old tumble-down hut – and do you know, there was a whole lot of machinery there. I don't know what it was – I've never seen anything like it before. Whatever do you think those men keep it there for? Seems funny, doesn't it, in a place like this?'

Tom sat up with a jerk. 'Some sort of *machinery*!' he said in amazement. 'What, in that old hut on that desolate mountainside, where there are only a few sheep? How would they get machinery there? There's no road.'

'There's a rough road the other side of the mountain,' said Sandy. 'Easy enough to go over the top, and get down to the path that way – and there's a good motor-road a bit further down the other side, too.'

Tom whistled. His eyes grew bright. 'I wonder if we've hit on something peculiar!' he said. 'We'll tell your father, and see what he says. Perhaps those two men are spies!'

'Don't be silly,' said Sandy. 'What would spies do here, among the mountains? There's nothing to spy on! Anyway, my father is away now.'

'All right, Mr Know-all,' said Tom. 'But we might as well tell your father when he comes back, all the same!'

CHAPTER 3

A CHAPTER OF QUARRELS

The next day the children began lessons with Miss Mitchell. Tom was most disgusted.

'Have I got to learn from a woman?' he said. 'I've been used to going to a boys' school. I don't want to learn from a woman.'

'Well, Sandy does,' said Mrs MacLaren with a laugh. 'And he's a pretty hefty boy, isn't he? There is no school here, you see, and until the war is over Sandy must stay at home.'

So Tom and Sheila joined Sandy and Jeanie in the schoolroom with Miss Mitchell – and they soon found a way of paying back the two Scottish children for the long walk of the day before! Tom was far ahead of Sandy in arithmetic, and Sheila's writing was beautiful – quite different from Jeanie's scrawl.

'Good gracious! Is that as far as you've got in arithmetic!' said Tom, looking at Sandy's book. 'I did those sums *years* ago! You *are* a baby!'

Sandy scowled down at his book. He knew he was not good at arithmetic. Miss Mitchell had struggled with him for years.

'Go to your place, Tom,' said Miss Mitchell briskly. 'Everybody isn't the same. Some are good at one thing and some are good at another. We'll see if your geography is as good as your arithmetic! Perhaps it isn't!'

But it was! Tom was a clever boy, and Sheila was a sharp little girl, who read easily and beautifully, and who wrote as well as Miss Mitchell herself.

'I can see that Sheila and I are going to be the top of the class!' said Tom slyly to Sandy, as they went out at eleven o'clock for a break in their lessons. 'You may be able to beat us at climbing mountains, Sandy – but we'll beat you at lesson-time! Why, Jeanie writes like a baby!'

'I *don't*!' said Jeanie, almost in tears.

'Yes, you do,' said Sheila. 'Why, at home even the *first* class could write better than you can! And you don't even know your twelve times table yet!'

This was quite true. Jeanie did not like lessons, and she had never troubled to try really hard to learn all her tables. Poor Miss Mitchell had been in despair over her many times.

But Jeanie was not going to have her English

cousins laughing at her. She made up her mind to learn all her tables perfectly as soon as she could. This was hard for her, because Jeanie would not usually spend any of her playtime doing anything but climbing the hills, swimming in the river, and driving round the lanes in the pony-trap or the waggonette.

Secretly Miss Mitchell was pleased that Tom and Sheila were ahead of Jeanie and Sandy. Now perhaps her two pupils would feel ashamed, and would work much harder.

'And it won't do Tom and Sheila any harm to find that they can't do the walking and climbing that our two can,' thought Miss Mitchell. 'After a few quarrels they will all settle down and be happy together.'

The two dogs eyed one another and tried to boast to one another in their own way. Paddy could do plenty of tricks, and whenever he wanted a biscuit he sat up on his hind legs in a comical way. Then Tom would put a biscuit on his nose, and say, 'Trust, Paddy, trust!'

Paddy would not eat the biscuit until Tom said 'Paid for!' Then he would toss the biscuit into the air, catch it, and gobble it up.

Mack watched this trick scornfully. *He* wasn't going to do any tricks for *his* food! Not he! If he wanted anything extra he'd go out and catch a rabbit. He was very proud of the fact that he could run as fast as a rabbit, and had three times brought a rabbit home to Sandy. Could Paddy do that? Mack barked to Paddy and asked him.

Paddy didn't answer. He lay curled up by Tom's feet, his eyes on Mack, ready to fly at him if he came any nearer. Mack whined scornfully, and then got up. He meant to show Paddy what he could do.

'Woof?' he said. Paddy got up too. He knew that Mack wanted him to go out with him, and though he was still on his guard, he thought it would be fun to go into the hills with this dog, who knew the way about.

'Look at that!' said Sandy in surprise. 'That's the first time that Paddy has gone with Mack without flying at him.'

The two dogs trotted out of doors, Paddy a good way behind. He could see the tiniest wag in Mack's tail and so he trusted him – but if that wag stopped, then Paddy was ready to pounce on him!

Out of the corner of his eye Mack saw Paddy's tail too. He could see the tiniest wag there also. Good. As long as that little wag was there, Mack knew that Paddy would not fling himself on him!

So, each watching the other carefully, the dogs went out on the hills. And then Mack began to show off to Paddy. He spied a rabbit under a bush and gave chase. The rabbit tore down a burrow. Mack started up another one and that went down a burrow too. Then Paddy started up a young rabbit, but it was away and up the hill before he had even seen which way it went!

'Woof! Watch me!' barked Mack, and he tore after a big rabbit so fast that he snapped at its white bobtail before it could get down a burrow. Mack walked back to Paddy, with the bit of white fluff still in his mouth.

Paddy turned his head away, pretending not to look, and then began to scratch himself. *He* wasn't going to tell this boastful dog that he thought it was jolly clever to catch a rabbit's tail – though secretly he couldn't help admiring Mack very much for his speed and strength. After he had scratched himself well, he got up and trotted back to the house.

'I'm tired of this silly game,' his tail seemed to say to Mack. Mack followed him in, disappointed. Paddy waited till both dogs were in the room, and then he stood on his hind legs and shut the door! This was another of his tricks, and people always thought it was very clever.

'Goodness! Did you see Paddy shut the door?' said Jeanie, quite astonished. 'Mack! *You* can't do that, old boy! You'd better learn!'

Mack was angry. He growled. What! Here he had just been smart enough to catch a rabbit's tail – and now this silly dog had shut the door and been praised for a stupid thing like *that*. Dear me – and Sheila was giving him a biscuit for his cleverness! Well, why didn't Sandy give *him* a biscuit for his smartness with rabbits?

And so both the dogs and the children were angry with the other's boasting, and would not be friends. Out-of-doors the Scottish cousins were far and away better than the English pair, and could run faster, jump higher and climb further – but indoors Tom and Sheila shone. Their lessons were done more quickly and better than their cousins', and they could learn anything by heart in a few minutes.

'It takes me half an hour to learn this bit of poetry,' grumbled Sandy. He was bent over 'Horatius keeps the Bridge'. He liked the story in it, but it was so difficult to learn.

'How slow you are!' laughed Tom. 'It took me just five minutes. I can say it straight off now – listen!'

'Oh be quiet, you boaster!' growled Sandy, putting his hands over his ears. 'I wish you'd never come! You make Miss Mitchell think that Jeanie and I are as stupid as sheep, and she's always scolding us.'

There was silence. Tom and Sheila said nothing at all. Sandy began to feel uncomfortable. He looked up. Tom had gone very red, and Sheila looked as if she was going to cry.

Tom got up and spoke stiffly. 'I'm sorry you wish we'd never come. We didn't think we were as bad as all that. But seeing that you have said what you really thought, I'll also say what *I* think. I wish we had never come too. Sheila and I have done our best to keep up with you in your walking and climbing because we didn't want you to think we were weak and feeble. But we are not used to mountains and it would have been kinder of you if you'd let us go a bit slower at first. However, I suppose that's too much to expect.'

'And *I'd* like to say something too!' burst out Sheila. 'You're always boasting about your wonderful mountains and the brown bur-r-rns, and the purple heather-r-r-r – but we would rather have the things we know. We'd like to see the big London buses we love, and our tall policemen, and to see the trains. We'd like to see more people about, and to go in the parks and play with our own friends at the games we know. It's p-p-p-perfectly horrid b-b-being here – and I w-w-w-want my m-m-m-mother!'

She burst into tears. Jeanie was horrified. Had they really been as unkind as all that? She ran over to Sheila and tried to put her arms round her cousin. But Sheila pushed her away fiercely. Tom went over and hugged his sister.

'Cheer up,' he said. 'When the war's over we'll go back home. Sandy and Jeanie will be glad to

be rid of us then – but we'll make the best of it till we go.'

Sandy wanted to say a lot of things but he couldn't say a word. He was ashamed of himself. After all, his cousins were his guests. How *could* he have said to them that he wished they had never come? What would his mother and father say if they knew? Scottish people were famous for the welcome they gave to friends.

Tom thought that Sandy was sulking, and he looked at him in disgust. 'I'm sorry Sheila and I are a bit more forward in our lessons than you,' he said. 'But we can't help that any more than you can help knowing your old mountains better than we do. Sheila, do stop crying. Here comes Aunt Jessie.'

Jeanie looked up in alarm. If Mother came in and wanted to know why Sheila was crying and found out – my goodness, there would be trouble! She and Sandy would be sent to bed at once, and have nothing but bread and water!

Sheila stopped crying at once. She bent her head over her book. Tom went to his place and began to mutter his poetry to himself – so when Mother came into the room she saw four children all working hard, and did not know that two of them were ashamed and frightened, that one was angry and hurt and the fourth one was very miserable and homesick.

She looked round. 'What, still doing lessons!' she said.

'It's some poetry Miss Mitchell gave us to learn before we went out,' explained Tom. 'We've nearly finished.'

'Well, finish it this evening,' said Mother. 'It's half-past two now, and a lovely day. Would you all like to take your tea out somewhere on the hills, and have a picnic? You won't be able to do it much longer, when the mists come down.'

'Oh yes, Mother, do let's have a picnic!' cried Jeanie, flinging down her book. She always loved a picnic. 'We'll go and find some blackberries.'

'Very well,' said Mother. 'Go and get ready and I'll pack up your tea.'

She went out. Jeanie spoke to Sheila. 'It was nice of you not to let Mother see you were crying,' she said. Sheila said nothing. She looked miserably at Jeanie. She did not want to climb mountains for a picnic. But there was no help for it. It was such a hilly country that sooner or later you had to climb, no matter in what direction you went!

The girls went to their room. Jeanie pulled out some comfortable old shoes and took them to Sheila. 'Look,' she said. 'Wear these, Sheila. They are old and strong, much better for climbing than the shoes you wear. Mother is getting some strong shoes for you next time she goes into the town.'

They fitted Sheila well. Jeanie gave her an old tammy instead of a straw hat. Then they went downstairs to find the boys.

Sandy still hadn't said a word to Tom. He just couldn't. He always found it very difficult to say he was sorry about anything. But he found a good stick and handed it to Tom, knowing that it would make climbing a good deal easier.

Tom took it – but he put it in a corner of the room when Sandy was not looking! He would dearly have loved to take it, but he wasn't going to have Sandy thinking he needed a stick, like an old man! Jeanie saw him put the stick away and she went to Sandy.

'Sandy!' she whispered. 'Tom would like the stick, I know, and so would Sheila – but they won't have them if they think we don't take them too. So let's take one each, and then the others won't mind.'

This was rather clever of Jeanie! For as soon as Tom saw that Jeanie and Sandy had also found sticks for themselves he at once went to take his from the corner where he had put it! After all, if his cousins used a stick, there was no reason why he shouldn't as well!

They set off. They allowed both dogs to come, for although they were still not good friends the two dogs put up with one another better now.

Tom and Sandy carried a bag each on their backs, full of the picnic things.

'I say! Let's go up to that funny old hut again, and see if those two men are still there!' said Tom, who always liked an adventure. 'I'd like to peep into that back room if I could, and find that machine that Sandy saw.'

'But isn't that too far?' said Jeanie, anxious to show that she could consider others. Tom shook his head stoutly. He was beginning to get used to the hills now.

'I can help Sheila over the bad bits,' he said, 'and now that she's got strong shoes on, and a good stick, she'll be all right, won't you, Sheila?'

'Yes,' said Sheila bravely – though her heart sank at the thought of the long climb again.

'All right then,' said Sandy. 'We'll go up to the hut and see what we can find!'

CHAPTER 4

A WALK AND A SURPRISE

They set off. Sheila did not find the climb so hard as she thought. She was getting used to walking in the hilly country now, and besides, Jeanie's shoes were well-made for climbing and were very comfortable. So Sheila walked well, and began to enjoy herself.

'We'll have our tea when we get to that clump of birch trees,' said Jeanie, when they had climbed for some time. 'There's a marvellous view from there. We can see the steamers going by, it's such a clear day!'

So, when they reached the birches, they all sat down and undid the picnic bags. There were tomato sandwiches, hard-boiled eggs, with a screw of salt to dip them into, brown bread and butter, buttered scones, and some fine currant cake. The children ate hungrily, and looked far away to where the sea shone blue in the autumn sunshine.

'There goes a steamer!' said Jeanie, pointing to where a grey steamer slid over the water. 'And there's another.'

'Over there is where the *Yelland* went down,' said Sandy, pointing to the east. 'And not far from it the *Harding* was torpedoed too. I hope those steamers will be all right that we are watching now.'

'Of course they will,' said Tom lazily. 'I bet there's no submarine round about here!'

Jeanie cleared up the litter and packed the bits of paper back into the bags. Her mother was always very strict about litter, and it had to be brought back and burnt, never left lying about.

'Well, what about creeping up to see if we can spot what's in that back room?' said Tom, getting up. 'I'm well rested now. What about you, Sheila?'

'Sheila can stay here with me,' said Jeanie, quickly. 'I don't want to go any further today. We'll wait here till you come back.'

Sheila looked at Jeanie gratefully. She was tired, and did not really want to go any further – but she would not have said so for anything!

Sandy looked at Jeanie in amazement, and was just going to tease her for being lazy, when his sister winked quickly at him. That wink said as plainly as anything – 'Sheila's tired but won't say so – so I'll pretend I am, and then she won't mind staying here.'

'All right, Jeanie,' said Sandy. 'Tom and I will go – and we'll take the two dogs.'

So off went the two boys, each with his stick, though Sandy kept forgetting to use his, and tucked it under his arm. Tom was glad to have the help of his, though, and it made a great difference to the climb.

When they had almost come in sight of the old cottage, Tom stopped. 'I think one of us had better stay here a few minutes with the dogs,' he said. 'The other can creep through the heather and find out whether the men are about – and that dog they spoke of. *I* don't want to be a dog's dinner!'

'All right,' said Sandy. 'Take the dogs, Tom. I'll go. I know the way better than you do.'

So Tom held the two dogs, and Sandy wriggled through the heather silently until he came in sight of the old cottage. No one seemed to be about. The door was shut. No dog barked.

Sandy wriggled closer. Not a sound was to be heard. No smoke came from the chimney. Sandy suddenly got up and ran to the old cottage. He peered in at the front window. The place was empty, though the furniture was still there.

It only took the boy a minute or two to make sure that no one, man or dog, was about. He ran to the edge of the heather and whistled to Tom. Up he came with the two dogs.

'There's no one here,' said Sandy. 'We'll go in and I'll show you that funny machinery with all its knobs and handles and things.'

They tried the door. It was locked! Sandy put his hefty shoulder to it and pushed — but the lock was good and strong and would not give an inch.

'They've put a new lock on it,' said the boy in disappointment. 'It never used to have a lock at all. Well, let's go and look in through the back window.'

They went round to the back of the cottage. But there they had a surprise!

'They've boarded up the window inside!' said Sandy in amazement. 'We can't see a thing! Not a thing! Oh blow! I did want to show you what was in that little room, Tom.'

'It's funny,' said Tom thoughtfully, rubbing his chin and frowning. 'Why should they do that? It means that the machinery, whatever it is, is still in there, and they've boarded it up in case we come back and spy around. I do wish we could get into the house.'

But it was no good wishing. The door was locked and bolted, the one front window was fastened tightly, and the back one was boarded up so well that not even a chink was left for peeping.

'Well, we can't see anything, that's certain,' said Tom. 'Let's go and have a look at that stream coming out of the hillside through that rock, Sandy. I'd like to see that again.'

The boys went there. The water still poured out of the curious hole – but there was not so much of it as before.

'That's because we haven't had so much rain this week,' explained Sandy. Tom nodded. He went to the hole and peered into it. 'If the water goes down much more we could easily get in there,' he said. 'I'd love to see where that water comes from. I read a book written by a Frenchman, Sandy, who explored heaps of underground streams and caves in France, and crawled through holes like that.'

'What did he find?' asked Sandy, interested.

'He found wonderful caves and underground halls and pits, and he found where some mysterious rivers had their beginnings,' said Tom. 'I'll show you the book when we get home. You know, if only we could get past that spring pouring out from the rock, we might find extraordinary caverns where no foot had ever trodden before!'

Tom was getting excited. His eyes shone, and he made Sandy feel thrilled too. 'Might there be a cave or something in this mountain then?' he asked.

'There might be heaps,' said Tom. 'And maybe somewhere in this great mountain is the beginning of the River Spelter. You told me that it comes out from underground and that no one knows where it rises.'

Sandy's eyes shone now. This was the most exciting thing he had ever heard of. 'Tom, we *must* explore this,' he said. 'We must! If only those men weren't here – they will send us away if they see us. I wish I knew what they were up to.'

'So do I,' said Tom. 'When your father comes back, we'll tell him about them, Sandy, and about the odd machinery they've hidden in that back room.'

A rabbit suddenly appeared on the hillside and looked cheekily at the two dogs, who were sitting quietly by the boys. At once both Paddy and Mack barked loudly and tore at the rabbit.

It did a strange thing. It shot up the hillside, leapt over the boys, and then disappeared into a burrow just beside the spring that gushed from the rock. And then Paddy did an even stranger thing!

He shot after the rabbit – but was stopped by the water. He leapt right over the water, saw the hole in the rock through which the spring flowed – and shot into the hole! He thought the rabbit had gone there!

He didn't come out. He disappeared completely. The two boys gaped at one another, and then Tom called his dog sharply.

'Paddy! Paddy! Come here!'

No Paddy came. Only a frightened whining could be heard from inside the hole. Paddy must have got right through the water and be sitting somewhere beyond.

'Paddy! Come out!' cried Tom anxiously. 'You got in – so you can get out! Come on now!'

But Paddy was terrified. The noise of the water inside the rock was tremendous, and the dog was terribly afraid. He had managed to scramble to a rocky shelf above the flow of the spring, and was sitting there, trembling. He could hardly hear the shouts of his master, because of the noise the water made.

'*Now* what are we to do?' said Tom, in dismay. 'He's right inside that rock. Paddy! PADDY, you idiot!'

But Paddy did not appear. Sandy looked worried. They must get the dog somehow.

Tom looked at Sandy. 'Well, I suppose he will come out sometime,' he said. 'Had we better wait any longer? The girls will be getting worried.'

'We can't leave your dog,' said Sandy. He knew that Tom loved Paddy as much as he loved Mack. Mack was looking astonished. He could not imagine where Paddy had gone!

Sandy climbed up to the rock, and looked into the hole. The rushing water wetted him, and spray flew into his face.

'I believe I could wriggle through the water today,' he said. 'It's not very deep and not very strong. I could find old Paddy and push him out for you.'

'Oh no, Sandy,' said Tom. 'You'd get soaked, and you might hurt yourself. You don't know what's behind that spring!'

Sandy was stripping off his clothes. He grinned at Tom. 'I don't mind if I *do* get soaked now,' he said. 'I'll just hang myself out to dry, if I do!'

CHAPTER 5

A RESCUE AND A
STRANGE DISCOVERY

Sandy climbed right up to the hole again, and then began to push himself into it. It was more than big enough for his body. As he wriggled, the cold water soaked him, and sometimes his face was under the surface, so that he had to hold his breath. His body blocked up the light that came in from the hole, and everything looked black as night. It was very strange.

He felt about as he went through the hole. It widened almost at once, behind the opening, and became higher and more spacious. The water became shallower too. Sandy sat up in the water, and felt about with his hand. He felt the rocky ceiling a little above him, and on one side was a rocky shelf. His hand touched wet hair!

'Paddy!' he cried. 'You poor thing! Go on out of the hole, you silly!'

His voice was almost drowned in the sound of the rushing water around him, but Paddy heard it and was comforted. He jumped down into the water beside Sandy. Sandy pushed him towards the hole.

Paddy was taken by the swirl of the water and lost his balance. The water took him like a floating log and he was rushed to the opening, struggling with all his feet. He shot out with the spring, and fell at Tom's feet.

Tom was delighted. He picked up the wet dog and hugged him, and then Paddy struggled down to shake the water from his hair. Mack came up and sniffed him in astonishment.

'Been swimming?' he seemed to say. 'What an extraordinary idea!'

Sandy was still in the rocky hole. He was getting used to the darkness now. He sat up on the shelf where he had found Paddy, and felt about with his hands. Then he made his way a little further up the stream. The rocky ceiling got quickly higher – and then Sandy found himself in a great cave, at the bottom of which the stream rushed along with a noise that echoed all around. It was so dark that Sandy could hardly see the shape of the cave. He only sensed that it rose high and was wide and spacious. He was filled with astonishment and excitement, and went back to tell Tom.

But meanwhile something was happening outside! Tom had heard voices, and, peeping

round the bend, he had seen in the distance the two men returning to their cottage! With them was a large dog.

Tom called in through the hole. 'Sandy! Sandy! Quick! Come back!'

Sandy was already coming back. He sat down in the water when the ceiling fell low, and then, as it became lower still, the boy had to lie full length in the water, and wriggle along like that, the stream sometimes going right over his face. He got to the opening at last, and Tom helped him down.

'Sandy! Hurry! The men are back!' whispered Tom. 'They've got a dog too, and he may hear us at any moment. Put on your things quickly.'

Sandy tried to be quick. But his body was cold from the icy water, and he could not make his hands pull on his things quickly over his wet body. He shook and shivered with the cold, and Tom did his best to help him to dress.

He was just getting on his coat when the men's dog came sniffing round the corner! When he saw the boys and the dogs he stood still, and the fur on his neck rose high with rage! He barked loudly.

'Quick!' said Tom to Sandy. 'We must go. Let's go down this way and maybe the men won't see us!'

So the two boys hurried round a bend, where

bracken grew tall, and began to make their way through it. The dog still barked loudly, and the two men came running to him.

'What is it? Who is it?' cried one of them. 'Go on, find him, find him!'

The fat man shouted something too, but the boys could not understand what he said. They were creeping down the hillside, glad that the men had not yet seen them. But the dog heard them, and came bounding after them.

'Now we're done for!' groaned Tom, as he saw the big dog leaping down towards them. He grasped his stick firmly. But someone else stood before him! It was Paddy, his wet fur bristling, and his throat almost bursting with fierce growls. Mack joined him, his teeth bared. Side by side the two dogs glared at the enemy, who, when he saw two of them, stopped still and considered. He was bigger than either – but they were two!

The men were following their dog. 'Come on, Tom,' whispered Sandy. 'Let the dogs settle it for us. We must get back to the girls quickly.'

They wriggled through the bracken and heather, slid down a stony piece unseen, and then made their way to where the girls were waiting anxiously. The boys had been a very long time.

'Sh!' said Sandy, as Jeanie opened her mouth to shout a welcome. And just as he said that a tremendous noise broke out – a noise of barking and howling and whining and yelping and growling and snarling!

'Good gracious!' said Jeanie, starting up. 'Are the dogs fighting?'

'Yes – fighting a big dog together!' said Sandy. 'Come on, we must go whilst the dogs are keeping off the men. They haven't seen us yet and we don't want them to.'

'But will the dogs be all right?' panted Sheila as they ran down the hillside.

'Of course!' said Sandy. 'Our Mack is more than a match for two other dogs, and I reckon your Paddy is too!'

The children stopped when they reached a big gorse bush, and sat down behind it, panting. They were safe there, for an old shepherd's shelter was nearby, and Loorie, the shepherd, was pottering about in the distance. In a few hurried words the boys told the girls all that had happened.

Tom stared when Sandy told of the cave behind the rock where the spring gushed out. 'I was right then!' he cried. 'I say, what fun! We must go and explore that when we get a chance. If only those men weren't there.'

'Perhaps they won't be there long, once my father hears about them,' said Sandy grimly. 'I think they are spies of some sort. I guess the police would like to see what is in their back room too!'

'I wish those dogs would come back,' said Sheila, looking worried, for she hated to think that Paddy might be bitten by the big dog.

No sooner had she spoken than the two dogs appeared, looking extremely pleased with themselves! Paddy's right ear was bleeding, and Mack's left ear looked the worse for wear – but otherwise they seemed quite all right.

They trotted up to the children together, and sat down, looking proud and pleased. Mack licked Paddy's ear. Paddy sniffed in a friendly way at Mack and then, putting out a paw, pawed him as if he wanted a game.

'Why, they're good friends now!' cried Jeanie in surprise. 'They like each other!'

Tom and Sandy looked at one another. Jeanie looked at Sheila.

'It's time *we* were friends too,' said Tom, with a red face. 'Thanks, Sandy, for rescuing Paddy from that hole. It was jolly good of you – getting into that icy-cold water and wriggling up a narrow rocky hole. You're a good sort.'

'So are you,' said Sandy. 'I'm sorry for what I said. I didn't mean it. I was only mad because you were better at arithmetic than I was. I'm glad you came, really.'

'Shake!' said Tom, with a laugh, and he held

out his hand to Sandy. 'We're friends now, and we'll stick by each other, won't we – just like the two dogs!'

The girls stared at the boys, glad to see that they were friends now. Jeanie held out her hand to Sheila. She would have liked to hug her, but she thought it looked grander to shake hands like the boys. Sheila solemnly shook her hand, and then they all began to laugh.

CHAPTER 6

A DISAPPOINTMENT – AND A PICNIC

Things began to happen very quickly after that exciting day. For one thing Captain MacLaren, Sandy's father, returned home on forty-eight hours' leave, and the children and Mrs MacLaren told him about the mysterious men in the old cottage on the mountain.

Captain MacLaren was astonished and puzzled. He was inclined to think that Sandy was making too much of the curious 'machinery' he had seen in the back room. However, when he heard that one man had called the other 'Carl,' he decided that he had better tell the police.

'Carl is a German name,' he said. 'I can't imagine why German spies could possibly want to hide themselves away on such a lonely hillside, but you never know! They may be up to something odd. I'll ring up the police.'

He did so – and two solemn Scots policemen

180

came riding out to Kidillin House on their bicycles, with large notebooks and stumpy pencils to take down all the children said.

'We'll go up to the cottage and investigate, captain,' said the sergeant, shutting his notebook with a snap. 'It's a wee bit unlikely we'll be finding anything to make a noise about, but we'll go.'

They knew where the cottage was, and they set off to find it that afternoon. The children were very much excited. Miss Mitchell could hardly get them to do any sums, French, or history at all. Even her star pupil, Tom, made all kinds of silly mistakes, and when he said that there were 240 shillings in a pound, instead of 240 pence, the governess put down her pencil in despair.

'This won't do,' she said. 'You are not thinking of what you are doing. What *are* you thinking of?'

But the four children wouldn't tell her! They were thinking of the exciting cave that Sandy had discovered behind the stream! They hadn't said a word about this to the grown-ups, because they were afraid that if they did they might be forbidden to explore it – and how could they bear to promise such a thing?

'We'll tell Mother as soon as we know exactly what's behind that hole,' said Sandy. 'We'll take our torches, and we'll explore properly. We might find strange cave pictures done by men hundreds of years ago! We might find old stone arrowheads and all kinds of exciting things!'

Sandy had been reading Tom's book. This book told of the true adventures of a Frenchman in underground caves and rivers, and of all the wonderful pictures he had found drawn on the walls and ceilings of the hidden caves. Sandy was simply longing to do some exploring himself now.

Miss Mitchell decided that it was no use doing any more lessons until the policeman came back from the old cottage. She was feeling a bit excited herself, and guessed what the children's feelings must be like. So she told them to shut their books, and go to do some gardening. Sandy and Jeanie each had their own gardens, and Tom and Sheila had been given a patch too.

'It is time to dig up your old beans and to cut down your summer plants, Sandy,' said Miss Mitchell. 'Tom, you can help the gardener to sweep up the leaves. Sheila, you can help Jeanie to get down the beanpoles.'

The children ran off, shouting in joy. From the garden they would be able to see the policemen when they came down from the mountain.

'They'll have the two spies with them!' said Sandy.

'Yes, and maybe they'll be handcuffed together,' said Tom, sweeping up the leaves as if they were spies! 'I wonder if they'll make the dog a prisoner too!'

'I guess our two dogs gave him a rough time!' said Jeanie. She looked at Mack and Paddy, who were tearing round and round after each other. Jeanie had doctored their ears well, and they were almost healed already. She was very good with animals. 'They're jolly good friends now!' said Jeanie, pleased. 'I'm glad we don't have to tie up first one and then another.'

'I wonder how the police will get that machinery down the mountain,' said Tom, stopping his sweeping for a moment.

'Same way as it was got up, I expect!' said Sandy. 'On somebody's back! I expect it was taken up in pieces from the road the other side of the mountain.'

'Look!' said Sheila suddenly. 'Here come the policemen! Aunt! Uncle! Miss Mitchell! Here come the policemen.'

In great excitement the children ran to the gate. But to their disappointment they saw that the two policemen coming down the hillside were alone. The men were not with them!

'I wonder why,' said Tom.

'Perhaps they weren't there,' suggested Jeanie.

The policemen came up to Kidillin House and

smiled as the children rained questions on them. Only when Captain MacLaren came out to see them did they say what had happened.

'Yes, sir, there are two men there all right,' said the sergeant. 'They say that they left London because of their fear of air-raids, and took that little cottage for safety. I asked them to let me look all over it – and there's no machinery of any sort there. I think yon boy of yours must have imagined it. There's no place round the old cottage where they could hide anything either.'

'I *didn't* imagine it!' cried Sandy. 'I didn't!'

'Did any of the others see it?' asked the sergeant, looking at Tom, Sheila, and Jeanie.

'No,' they said. 'But we saw the windows boarded up!'

'They say they did that for the black-out,' said the second policeman. 'They've curtains for the front room but none for the back.'

'Pooh! As if they'd bother to black-out windows that look right on to the mountain behind!' said Tom, scornfully. 'All a made-up tale!'

'One man is deaf and dumb,' said the sergeant. 'We got all the talk from the dark man.'

That made the children stare even more. Both Tom and Sandy had heard the *two* men talking. Why then did one pretend to be deaf and dumb?

The policemen jumped on to their bicycles and rode off, saluting the captain. The children gathered together in a corner of the garden and began to talk.

'What have they done with the machinery?'

'Why did one pretend to be dumb?'

'What a stupid reason for boarding up the window!'

'I guess I know why one pretended to be dumb! I bet he talks English with a German accent! I bet if he answered the policeman's questions, he would give himself away at once!' This was Tom speaking, and the others listened to him.

'Yes, that's it!' went on the excited boy. 'He's the one called Carl – he's a German all right. It's an old trick to pretend to be dumb if you don't want to give yourself away!'

'And they guessed we might tell the police so they hid their machinery quickly,' said Sandy. 'But didn't have time to unboard the windows.'

'That's it,' said Tom. There was a silence, whilst they all thought quickly.

'Golly! I think I know!' cried Tom, in such an excited voice that they all jumped. 'They've taken it to pieces, and managed somehow to get it into the cave behind the stream! That's what they've done. Somehow or other they must have known about that cave.'

'It would be easy enough to do that, if the two of them worked together,' said Sandy, thinking hard. 'They could wrap the pieces in oiled cloth, tie them to ropes – and then one man could climb back to the cave and pull up the rope whenever the other man tied the packets on to it. It is sure to be able to break down into pieces, that machine – how else could they have got it up to the cottage so secretly?'

'We've hit on their secret all right,' said Tom, and his face glowed. '*Now* what we've got to do is quite simple.'

'What's that?' asked all the others.

'Why, all we've got to do is to go up to the cottage, lie low till the men go shopping or something, and then explore that cave again,' said Tom. 'If we find the machinery is there, we'll know we're right, and we can slip down to the police at once!'

'Oh good!' said Sandy. 'The girls could keep watch for us, Tom, and you and I could take our swim-suits and wriggle through the hole together.'

'Is there time today?' wondered Tom looking at his watch. But there wasn't. It was a nuisance, because all the children were longing to go on with their big adventure – and now they would have to wait till the next day!

Fortunately for them the next day was

Saturday. They begged their governess to let them take their lunch on the hills. Mrs MacLaren had gone to the town to see her husband off once more, and Miss Mitchell was in charge.

'Very well,' said Miss Mitchell. 'I think I'll come with you today. I've nothing much to do.'

The children stared at one another in dismay. If Miss Mitchell came they couldn't do anything! They could not think of a single reason to give her to stop her coming.

'I'll go and ask the cook to get a good lunch ready,' said Miss Mitchell, bustling out to the kitchen. 'I'll pack it up nicely in the picnic bags.'

'Well, isn't that awful!' said Sheila, as the governess went out of the room. 'What *can* we do to stop her coming?'

They thought and thought – but it was no good. She would have to come!

'Well, listen,' said Tom at last. 'After we have had our picnic, you two girls can stay with Miss Mitchell, and Sandy and I will slip off to explore again. That's the only thing we can do.'

'But we wanted to come too!' wailed Sheila.

'Well, you can't!' said Tom. 'Now for goodness' sake don't make a fuss, Sheila, or Miss Mitchell will begin to think something's up!'

But Miss Mitchell didn't guess anything at

187

all. She packed up the lunch, gave it to the two boys to carry on their backs, and soon they were all ready to start.

'Got your torch, Sandy?' whispered Tom.

'Yes,' whispered back Sandy. 'And I've got my swim-suit on under my clothes too!'

They all set off. They climbed up the sunny hillside, chattering and laughing, picking black-berries as they went. Miss Mitchell was glad to see them all such good friends now, even the two dogs! They chased rabbits, real and imaginery, all the time, and once Paddy got so far down a hole that he had to be pulled out by Tom.

The boys made their way towards the cottage. Miss Mitchell was not sure she wanted to go there.

'Those men won't like us spying around,' she said. 'They probably guess that it is you children who had the police sent up there.'

'Well, we'll not go too near,' said Sandy. 'What about having our lunch here, Miss Mitchell? There's a beautiful view for you to look at.'

Miss Mitchell knew the view well. It was the same one that the children had looked at before, when they watched the steamers going by, far away on the blue sea. They all sat down, glad of a rest.

'There's a steamer,' said Tom.

'Yes,' said Miss Mitchell, looking at it through the pair of field-glasses she had brought. 'I hope it won't be sunk. Those coastal steamers should go in convoys, but they won't be bothered – and two were sunk the other day.'

'What were they?' asked Sandy. 'The *Yelland* and the *Harding*, do you mean?'

'No, two others have been sunk since then,' said Miss Mitchell. 'By a submarine too – so there must be one lurking about somewhere.'

The children looked at the little steamer slipping slowly along, and hoped that it would not be sunk. Miss Mitchell opened the picnic bags and handed out ham sandwiches, tomatoes, hard-boiled eggs, apples, jam-tarts and ginger buns.

'Ooooh! What a gorgeous picnic!' said Sheila, who was rapidly getting as big an appetite as her Scottish cousins. There was creamy milk to drink too. The dogs had one large biscuit each and little bits of ham that the children pulled from their sandwiches. Everybody was very happy.

'Goodness me, the sun's hot!' said Miss Mitchell, after they had all eaten as much as they could. 'You had better have a little rest before we go on – we really can't climb higher, on top of our enormous lunch!'

She lay back on the warm heather and put her hat over her eyes. The children sat as still as mice. The same thought came into everyone's head. Would Miss Mitchell go to sleep?

For five minutes nobody said a single word. Even the dogs lay quiet. Then Jeanie gave a little cough. Miss Mitchell didn't stir. Jeanie spoke in a low voice. 'Miss Mitchell!'

No answer from Miss Mitchell. Jeanie leaned over her governess, and lifted Miss Mitchell's hat up gently so that she could see if the governess was really asleep.

Her eyes were fast shut and she was breathing deeply. Jeanie nodded to the others. Very quietly they got up from the heather, shaking their fingers at the two dogs to warn them to be quiet. They climbed up higher, rounded a bend in the hillside, and then began to giggle.

'Good!' said Tom, at last. 'We've got away nicely. Now come on quickly, everyone. We haven't a minute to lose!'

They climbed quickly towards the old cottage, keeping a good look-out as they went. Would the two men be about? Would they be able to do any exploring? They all felt tremendously excited, and their hearts beat loudly and fast.

CHAPTER 7

MISS MITCHELL IS VERY CROSS

Slowly and quietly the children crept over the heather that surrounded the cottage. Mack and Paddy crept with them, joining in what they thought was some new game.

No one was about. The dog was not to be seen either. 'I'll just creep over to the cottage and see what I can see!' whispered Sandy. So off he went, running quietly to the hut. He peeped cautiously in at a window – and then drew back very quickly indeed.

He came back to the others. 'The two men are there,' he whispered. 'But they are sound asleep, like Miss Mitchell! This must be a sleepy afternoon! Come on – we'll go to the underground burn, and see if we can get into the cave and look round before the men wake up.'

In great delight the four children crept quietly off to where the big rock jutted out,

192

through which the water fell down the mountain-side. But when they came in sight of it, what a shock they got!

Tied up beside the rock was the big dog!

The children stopped in dismay. Tom pushed them back, afraid that the dog would see or hear them. They stared at one another, half-frightened.

'It's no good trying any exploring this afternoon!' said Tom, frowning in disappointment. 'Absolutely no good at all. But it shows one thing plainly – they're afraid we may guess their hiding-place and explore it – so they've put the dog there to guard it!'

'Well, we can't possibly get past that big brute,' said Sandy. 'I wonder now if there are any signs of trampling round about the burn there, Tom. If they've hidden anything in that cave, they'd have to stand around the rock a good bit, and the footmarks would show. I've a good mind to creep nearer and see.'

'No, let *me*,' said Tom at once. He always liked to be the one to do things if he could – and Sandy had done the exploring last time! Tom felt it was his turn.

'Tom! Come back!' whispered Sandy, as Tom crept forward on hands and knees. 'I can go much more quietly than you!'

But Tom would not turn back. It was a pity

he didn't – for suddenly he knelt on a dry twig which cracked in two like a pistol shot!

The dog, lying quietly by the rock, raised up its head at once and then leapt to its feet, sniffing the air. Tom crouched flat – but the dog saw him. It began to bark loudly, and the mountain-side rang and echoed with its loud voice.

'Quick! Get down the slope, back to Miss Mitchell!' said Sandy. 'Those men will be out in a minute!'

Sandy was right. The two men woke up at once when they heard the barking of the dog. The door of the cottage opened and out they ran. One of them shouted loudly. 'What is it, Digger, what it it?'

Then he saw the children disappearing down the hillside and with a cry of rage he followed them. 'Loose the dog!' he yelled to the other man. The children tore away as fast as they could, slipping and sliding as they went.

The dog was loosed – but as soon as he was faced once more by the two dogs who had beaten him the other day he dropped his tail and refused to go after the children. The man beat him, but it was no use. Digger was afraid of Mack and Paddy.

But the first man was not afraid of anything! He plunged down the hillside after the children, and just as they reached the place where they had left Miss Mitchell, he caught them up.

Miss Mitchell awoke in a hurry when she heard such a noise of scrambling and shouting. She sat up and looked round. The children ran up to her – and the man came up in a rage.

'What are these children doing here?' he shouted. 'I tell you, I'll whip them all if they come spying round here. Can't a man be left in peace?'

'I don't know what you are talking about,' said Miss Mitchell firmly. 'We came up on the hills for a picnic, and we have as much right here as you have. Please go away at once, or I will report you to the police.'

The man glared at Miss Mitchell. He began to shout again, but when Miss Mitchell repeated that she would certainly tell the police of his threats to her children, he muttered something and went back up the hillside.

Miss Mitchell was very angry with them. 'So you slipped off up to the cottage when I was having a little nap, did you?' she scolded. 'Now you see what has happened! You have made enough trouble for those two men already by telling made-up tales about them – and now you go prowling round their cottage again! You will promise me not to go there again.'

The children looked at one another in dismay. Just what they hoped wouldn't happen!

'Very well,' said Sandy sulkily. 'I promise not to go to the cottage again.'

'So do I,' said Tom. The girls promised too. Miss Mitchell gathered up the picnic things, and said that they must all return home. She really was very cross.

'Miss Mitchell, those weren't made-up tales,' said Sandy, as they went down the mountainside. 'You shouldn't say that. You know we speak the truth.'

'I don't want to hear any more about it,' said the governess. 'It is most unpleasant to have a man roaring and shouting at us like that, because of your stupid behaviour. You know quite well that I would not have allowed you to go to the cottage if you had asked me.'

Miss Mitchell was cross all that day. But the next day was better, and the children went to church glad that Miss Mitchell seemed to have forgotten about the day before. She had not told their mother about them, so that was good.

When they came out of church there was half an hour before lunch. In the distance the children saw Loorie, the old shepherd. Sandy was fond of him, and asked Miss Mitchell if they might go and talk to him.

Loorie was doctoring a sheep that had a bad leg. He nodded to the children, and smiled at Tom and Sheila when Sandy explained that they were his cousins.

'This is an easy time of year for you, isn't it, Loorie?' asked Sandy.

'Oh aye,' said the old man, rubbing the sheep's leg with some horrid-smelling black ointment. 'The winter's the busy time, when the lambing's on.'

He went on to tell Tom and Sheila of all the happenings of the year. The two town children listened in great interest. They could hardly understand the Scottish words the old man used, but they loved to hear them.

'Did you lose any lambs this year, Loorie?' asked Sandy.

'Aye, laddie, I lost too many,' said Loorie. 'And do you ken where I lost them? Down the old pot-hole on the mountain up there!'

'What old pot-hole?' asked Tom, puzzled.

'Oh, it's a peculiar place,' explained Sandy. 'There's a big hole up there, that goes down for ever so far. The sheep sometimes fall into it and they can never be got out.'

'It's funny to sit by the hole,' said Jeanie. 'You can hear a rushing sound always coming up it.'

'Folks do say that's the River Spelter,' said Loorie, setting the sheep on its legs again. 'Aye, folks say a mighty lot of things.'

'The Spelter!' said Tom, surprised. 'Why, do you mean that the Spelter goes under the pot-hole you're talking about?'

'Maybe it does and maybe it doesn't,' said the old shepherd, closing his tin of ointment. 'There's funny things in the mountains. Don't you go taking the lassies near that pot-hole, now, Master Sandy!'

'There's Miss Mitchell calling,' said Sandy hurriedly, for he saw by Tom's face that his cousin was longing to go to visit the pot-hole! 'Goodbye, Loorie. We'll see you again soon.'

As they ran back to Miss Mitchell, Tom panted out some questions. 'Where's the pot-hole? Is it anywhere near the underground stream? Do you suppose that's the Spelter that runs beneath the pot-hole, or our stream?'

Sandy didn't know at all. But he knew quite well that before that day was out, Tom would want to go and explore the pot-hole! Sandy wanted to as well.

'I can't think why I didn't remember the pot-hole before,' thought the boy. 'I suppose it was because I've known about it all my life and never thought anything about it.'

CHAPTER 8

DOWN THE POT-HOLE

That afternoon the four children and the dogs set off to the pot-hole. They had talked about it excitedly, and Tom felt sure that if there was water at the bottom, it might be the very same stream that poured out of the hole in the rock. If it was, they could get down the hole and follow it up – and maybe come to the cave from behind.

'And then we can see if the spies have hidden their things there!' cried Sandy. 'We didn't think there could be another way in – but there may be! What a good thing we had that talk to old Loorie this morning.'

They took a good many things with them that afternoon. Both boys had strong ropes tied round their waists. All of them had torches, and Tom had matches and a candle too.

'You see,' he explained, 'if the air is bad, we

200

can tell it by lighting a candle. If the candle flickers a lot and goes out, we shall know the air is too bad for us. Then we shall have to go back.'

They also had towels with them, because Tom thought they might have to undress and wade through water. They could leave their towels by the pot-hole and dry themselves when they came back. They all felt excited and important. They were out to catch spies, and to find out their secrets!

Sandy took them round the mountain, in the opposite direction to the one they usually went, and at last brought them to the pot-hole.

It certainly was a very odd place. It looked like a wide pit, overgrown with heather and brambles – but Sandy explained that when they climbed down into this pit-like dell, they would come to the real pot-hole, a much narrower pit at one side of the dell.

They climbed down into the dell, and Sandy took them to one side. He kicked away some branches, and there below them was the pot-hole!

'Loorie must have put those branches across to stop the sheep from falling in,' said Sandy. 'Now just sit beside this hole and listen.'

The four of them sat beside the strange hole. It was not very big, not more than a yard wide, and curious bits of blue slate stuck out all around it. The children peered down into the hole, but it was like looking down into an endless well. They could see nothing but blackness.

But they could hear a most mysterious noise coming up to them! It was like the sound of the wind in the trees, but louder and stranger.

'Yes — that's water rushing along all right,' said Tom, sitting up again, his face red with excitement. 'But it sounds to me a bigger noise than our little stream could make. It sounds more like the River Spelter rushing along in the heart of the mountain, down to where it flows out at the foot, in the village of Kidillin!'

'Could we possibly get down there?' asked Sandy doubtfully. 'Would our ropes be long enough? We don't want any accidents! I don't know how we'd be rescued!'

Tom flashed his torch down the hole. 'Look!' he said. 'Do you see down there, Sandy — about seven feet down? There's a sort of rocky shelf. Well, we may find that all the way down there are these rocky bits to help us. If we have a rope firmly round our waists so that we can't fall, we'll be all right. I'll go down first.'

'No, you won't,' said Sandy. 'I'm better used to climbing. Don't forget that it was you who cracked that twig yesterday and gave warning to the dog. If it had been I who was creeping along, the dog would never have known.'

Tom looked angry. Then the frown went from his face and he nodded. 'All right,' he said. 'Perhaps it would be best if you went. You're good at this sort of thing and I've never done it before.'

'The girls are not to come,' said Sandy. 'Not today, at any rate. It looks more dangerous than I thought, and anyway, we'll want someone to look after the ropes for us. We will tie the ends to a tree, and the girls can watch that they don't slip.'

Neither of the girls made any objection to being left at the top. Both of them thought the pot-hole looked horrid! They were quite content to let the boys try it first!

They all felt really excited. Sandy tied the ends of their two strong ropes to the trunk of a stout pine tree. He and Tom knotted the other ends round their waists as firmly as they could. Now, even if they fell, their ropes would hold them, and the girls could pull them up in safety!

Sandy went down the pot-hole first. He let himself slip down to the rocky ledge some way down. His feet caught on it with a jerk. His hands felt about for something to hold.

'Are you all right, Sandy?' asked Tom, flashing his torch down the hole.

'Yes,' said Sandy. 'I'm feeling to see if there's somewhere to put my feet further down.' Sandy was as good as a cat at climbing. He soon found a small ledge for his right foot, and then another for his left.

Bits of slate, stone and soil broke away as he slowly climbed downwards, and fell far below him. The pot-hole did not go straight down, but curved a little now and again, so that it was not so difficult as Sandy had expected to climb down.

'Come on, Tom!' he called. 'If you're careful where to put your feet, it's not too difficult.'

Tom began his climb down too. He found it far more difficult than Sandy, for he was not so used to climbing. His feet slithered and slipped, and he cut his hands when he clutched at stones and earth.

The girls at the top were holding on to the boys' ropes, letting them out gradually. Tom's rope jerked and pulled, but Sandy's rope went down smoothly.

As Sandy went down further and further, the noise of rushing water became louder and louder until he could not even hear his own voice when he called to Tom. Tom was kicking out so many stones and bits of earth that they fell round poor Sandy like a hailstorm!'

'Stop kicking at the sides of the hole!' yelled Sandy. But Tom couldn't help it. Sandy wished he had put on a hat, to stop the pebbles from hitting his head — but soon, at a bend in the hole, he became free of the 'hailstorm,' and went downwards comfortably.

It was the first part that was so steep and difficult. It was easier further down, for rocky ledges stuck out everywhere, making it almost like climbing down a ladder.

The noise of the water was deafening. Sandy thought it was so near that he might step into it at any moment. So he switched on his torch and looked downwards. The black water gleamed up at him, topped with white spray where it flowed over out-jutting rocks. It was further down than he had thought.

As he climbed down to the water, the hole widened tremendously, and became a cave. Sandy jumped down beside the shouting river, and stood there, half-frightened, half-delighted.

It was a strange sight, that underground river! It flowed along between rocky walls, black, strong and noisy. It entered the cave by a low tunnel, which was filled to the roof with the water. The river flowed in a rocky bed and entered another black tunnel just near Sandy — but it did not fill this tunnel to the roof. Sandy flashed his torch into the tunnel, and saw that for some way, at any rate, the roof was fairly high, about up to his head.

There was a rattle of stones about him, and

Tom came sliding down the walls of the pot-hole at a great speed! He had missed his footing and fallen! But he had not far to fall, and fortunately for him, his rope was only just long enough to take him beside Sandy, and it pulled him up with a jerk, before he fell into the water.

'Good gracious!' said Sandy. 'You *are* in a hurry!'

'Phew!' said Tom, loosening the rope a little round his waist. 'That wasn't very pleasant. I'm glad I was fairly near the bottom. My word, the rope did give my waist an awful pull! I say, Sandy! What a marvellous sight this is!'

'The underground world!' said Sandy, flashing his torch around. 'Look at that black rushing river, Tom! We've got to wade down that, through that tunnel – see?'

'Oooh!' said Tom. 'Where do you suppose it goes to?'

'That's what we've got to find out,' said Sandy. 'I think myself that away up that other tunnel there, is the source of the Spelter. It probably begins in a collection of springs all running to the same rocky bed in the mountain, and then rushing down together as a river. But really it's not more than a fast stream here, though it makes enough noise for a river!'

'That's because it is underground, and the echoes are peculiar,' said Tom. 'Also, it is going downhill at a good rate, not flowing gently in an even bed. How deep do you suppose it is, Sandy?'

'We'll have to find out!' said Sandy, beginning to undress. 'Hurry up! Got your torch with you? Well, bring it, and bring the oil-skin bag too, in case we have to swim, and need something waterproof to put our torches in. I've got the candles and matches.'

CHAPTER 9

IN THE HEART OF
THE MOUNTAIN

Both boys stood in their swim-suits. They shivered, for the air was cold. Sandy put one leg into the rushing stream. The water was icy!

'Oooh!' said Sandy, drawing back his leg quickly! 'It's mighty cold, Tom. Just hang on to me a minute, will you, so that I can feel how deep the water is.'

Tom held on to his arms. Sandy slipped a foot into the water again. He went in over his knee, and right up to his waist! Then he felt a solid rocky bottom, and stood up, grinning.

'It's all right!' he said. 'Only up to my waist, Tom. Come on in and we'll explore the tunnel.'

Tom got into the water, and then the two boys began to wade along the noisy stream. It went gradually downwards, and once there was quite a steep drop, making a small waterfall. The boys had to help one another down. It was very cold, for the water was really icy. They were both shivering, and yet felt hot with excitement.

The roof of the tunnel kept about head or shoulder-high. Once the tunnel widened out again into a small cave, and the boys climbed out of the water and did some violent exercises to warm themselves.

They got back into the water again. It suddenly got narrow and deeper. Deeper and deeper it got until the two boys had to swim. And then, oh dear the tunnel roof dipped down and almost reached the surface of the water!

'*Now* what are we to do?' said Tom, in dismay.

'Put your torch into its oil-skin bag, to begin with,' said Sandy, putting his into the bag, next to the candle and box of matches. 'Then it won't get wet. If you'll just wait here for me, Tom, I'll swim underwater a little way and see if the roof rises further on.'

'Well, for goodness' sake be careful,' said Tom, in alarm. 'I hope you've got enough breath to swim under the water *and* back, if the roof doesn't rise! The water may flow for a long way touching the roof.'

'If it does, we can go no further,' said Sandy. 'Don't worry about *me*! I can swim under water for at least a minute!'

He took a deep breath, plunged under the

water, and swam hard. He bobbed his head up, but found that the rocky ceiling still touched the stream. He went on a little way, and then, when he was nearly bursting for breath, he found that the roof lifted, and he could stand with his head out of the water.

He took another deep breath and went back for Tom. 'It's all right,' he gasped, coming up beside him. 'You need to take a jolly good breath though. Take one now and come along quickly.'

Tom began to splutter under the water before he could stick his head up into the air once more and breathe. Sandy couldn't help laughing at him, and Tom was very indignant.

'Just stop laughing!' he said to Sandy. 'I was nearly drowned!'

'Oh no you weren't,' giggled Sandy. 'I could easily have pulled you through, Tom. Come on – the next bit is easy. We can swim or wade. Let's swim and get warm.'

So they swam along in the deep black water for some way – and then the tunnel widened out into a great underground hall. It was an odd place. Strange stones gleamed in the light of their torches. Phosphorescent streaks shone in the rocky walls, and here and there curious things hung down from the ceiling rather like icicles.

'Ooh, isn't it odd?' whispered Tom – and at

once his whisper came back to him in strange echoes. 'Isn't it odd, isn't it odd – odd – odd?' The whole place seemed to be full of his whispering.

'It's magnificent!' said Sandy, revelling in the strangeness of it. 'See how those stones gleam? I wonder if they're valuable. And look at the shining streaks in that granite-like wall! I say, Tom, fancy – perhaps we are the very first people to stand in this big underground hall!'

The underground river split into three in the big cavern. One lot of water went downwards into the steep tunnel, one wandered off to the other end of the cavern, and the third entered a smaller tunnel, and ran gently along it as far as Sandy could see.

'We'll follow this second one that goes to the other end of the cave,' said Sandy. 'We needn't wade in it – we can walk beside it. Come on.'

So they walked beside it, and found that it wandered through a narrow archway into yet another cave – and there they saw a strange sight.

The water stopped there and formed a great underground lake, whose waters gleamed purple, green and blue by the light of the boys' torches. The lake was moved by quiet ripples. Tom and Sandy stood gazing at it.

'Isn't it marvellous?' whispered Tom, and

again his whisper ran all round and came back to him in dozens of echoes.

Sandy suddenly got out the candle and lit it. The flame flickered violently and almost went out.

'The air's bad in this cave!' cried Sandy. 'Come back to the other, where the rushing water is! Quick!'

He and Tom left the strange lake, and ran back to the great, shining hall. The air felt much purer at once and the boys took big breaths of it. The candle now burnt steadily.

'For some reason the air isn't good yonder,' said Sandy. 'Well, we can't go *that* way! There's only one way left – and that's to wade down that tunnel over there. Maybe it's the right one!'

'We'll hope so,' said Tom, doing some more exercises, and jumping up and down. 'Come on, Sandy. In we go!'

So into the water they went once more. How cold it was again! The tunnel was quite high above the water, and the stream itself was shallow, only up to their knees. It was quite easy to get along.

They waded along for a long way, their torches lighting up the tunnel. And then a very surprising thing happened.

They heard the murmur of voices! Tom and Sandy listened in the greatest astonishment.

Perhaps it was the noise of the stream? Or strange echoes?

They went on again, and came out into a small cave through which the stream flowed quite placidly. And there they heard the voices again!

Then suddenly the voices stopped, and an even more peculiar sound came. It was the sound of somebody playing an organ!

CHAPTER 10

A VERY STRANGE DISCOVERY

Sandy clutched hold of Tom, for the sound crept into every corner of the cave, and filled it full. They were drowned in music!

It went on and on and then stopped. No further noise came, either of voices or music. The boys flashed their torches into each other's faces and looked at one another in amazement.

'An organ! In the heart of the mountain!' said Tom, in an amazed whisper. 'Didn't it sound wonderful?'

'Come on — let's get out of this cave and see what's in the next one!' whispered Sandy. 'Maybe there's an underground church here, with somebody playing the organ!'

The boys crept along, one behind the other. They suddenly saw a light shining through a rugged opening in the cave. It came from a cave beyond. Sandy peeped round to see what it was.

A lantern swung from a rope in the roof of a cave. It was a large cave, and in it were the two men who lived in the old cottage! They were crouched over the machinery that Sandy had seen in the back room!

Sandy clutched Tom's hand, and his heart leapt and beat fast. So they had actually come to the cave behind the gushing spring that fell from the hole in the rock!

They could hardly believe their good luck! They squeezed each other's hand, and wished that the men would go away from the machinery, whatever it was, so that they might see what it was.

'I wish they'd go back to the cottage,' whispered Sandy – and at once his whisper ran round and round and sounded like a lot of snakes hissing! The men looked up in alarm.

'What was that noise?' said one.

The second man answered in a language that Sandy knew was German. He wasn't deaf and dumb then! Sandy rejoiced. They *were* spies, he felt quite sure. But how could he make them go away, so that he and Tom could examine the cave properly.

Sandy had an idea. He suddenly began to make the most dreadful moaning noises imaginable, like a dog in pain. He made Tom jump – but the two men jumped even more. They sprang up and looked round fearfully.

'Oooh, ah, ooh-ooh-ah, wee-oo, wee-oo, waaaah!' wailed Sandy. The echoes sent the groaning noise round and round the cave, gathering together and becoming louder and louder till the whole place was full of the wildest moaning and wailing you could imagine!

The men shouted something in fear. They ran to the stream, jumped into it, waded in the water till they got to the rock through which it flowed, and then wriggled out of the hole, down to the ground below, on the sunny hillside. They had never in their lives been so terrified.

Tom and Sandy screamed with laughter. They held on to one another, and laughed till they could laugh no more. And the echoes of their laughter ran all around them till it seemed as if the whole place must be full of laughing imps.

'Come on – let's have a look round now,' said Sandy at last. They ran into the men's cave – and then Tom saw what the 'machinery' was!

'It's a radio transmitter!' he cried. 'I've seen one before. These men can send out radio messages as well as receive them – and oh, Sandy, that's what they've been doing, the wretches! As soon as they see the steamers pass on the sea in the distance, they send a radio message to some submarine lurking near by, and the submarine torpedoes the steamers!'

'Oh! So that's why there have been so many steamers sunk round our coast,' said Sandy, his eyes flashing in anger. 'The hateful scoundrels! I'm going to smash their set, anyway!'

Before Tom could stop Sandy, the raging boy picked up a stone and smashed it into the centre of the transmitter. 'You won't sink any *more* steamers!' he cried.

'Good,' said Tom. 'Now let's wriggle to the hole where the stream gushes out, Sandy, and see if the men are anywhere near. If they're not, we could wriggle out, and go back to the girls overground. I really don't fancy going all the way back underground!'

'Nor do I,' said Sandy. 'It would be much quicker if we got out here, went up to the top of the mountain, and climbed down from there to where the girls are waiting.'

'Fancy, Sandy – we've been right through the mountain!' said Tom. 'I guess no boy has ever had such an adventure as we've had before!'

'Come on,' said Sandy. 'I'll go first.'

He was soon at the mouth of the hole. He peered out – but there was no one about at all, not even the big dog. 'I bet the men have run into the cottage, taken the dog to guard them, and locked the door!' called back Sandy.

'Well, your wails and groans were enough to

make anyone jump out of their skin!' said Tom.
'I got an awful scare myself, Sandy!'

The two boys wriggled out of the hole, soaked
again by the rushing water. But once they stood
in the warm sun they forgot their shivers and
danced for glee.

'Come on!' said Sandy. 'No time to lose! The
climb will make us as warm as can be!'

Off they went, climbing up the mountainside, revelling in the feel of the warm heather.
The sun shone down and very soon they were as
warm as toast – too warm, in fact, for Tom began
to puff and pant like an engine!

They went over the top at last, sparing a
moment to look back at the magnificent view.
Far away they could see the blue sea, with a
small steamer on it. 'The submarine can't be told
about *you*!' said Sandy. 'Come on, Tom.'

On they went. Tom followed Sandy, for Sandy
knew every inch of the way. Down the other side
they went, scrambling in their swim-suits over
the heather. And presently in the distance, they
saw the blue frocks of the two girls.

Sheila was bending anxiously over the pot-
hole, wishing the boys would come back. It was
so long now since they had gone down the hole.
She almost fell down it herself when she heard
Sandy's shout behind her.

'Hello! Here we are!'

The girls leapt to their feet and looked round in amazement. They were so surprised that they couldn't say a word. Then Jeanie spoke.

'How *did* you get out of the pot-hole?' she gasped. 'Sheila and I have been sitting here for hours, watching – and now you suddenly appear!'

'It's a long story,' said Sandy, 'but a very surprising one. Listen!'

He sat down on the heather and he and Tom told how they had made their way through the heart of the mountain, wading and swimming in the river, and how they had found the strange underground lake, and had taken the right turning to the cave behind the spring. When they told about the men, and how Sandy had frightened them with his groans and wails, the girls flung themselves backwards and squealed with laughter.

'And now we know the secret of why our steamers on this coast are so easily sunk,' finished Sandy. 'It's because of those two traitors and their radio. Well, I smashed that! And now the best thing we can do is to go back home and get the police again!'

'What about our clothes?' asked Tom.

'They can wait,' said Sandy. 'We'll get them from the pot-hole sometime. We ought to go and get the police before the men discover that I've broken their radio, and escape!'

'Come on then!' cried the girls, jumping up, 'We're ready!'

And down the hillside they all tore, the two boys in their swim-suits, with their oil-skin bags still hanging round their necks!

CHAPTER 11

THE HUNT FOR
THE TWO SPIES

Miss Mitchell jumped in surprise when the four children rushed into the garden where she was busy cutting flowers – the boys in their swim-suits, and the girls squealing with excitement.

'Miss Mitchell! Miss Mitchell! We've found out all about the two spies!'

'Miss Mitchell! We've been down the pot-hole!'

'Miss Mitchell! We know how those steamers were sunk!'

'Miss Mitchell! Can we phone the police? Listen, do listen!'

So Miss Mitchell listened, and could hardly believe her ears when the children told her such an extraordinary tale.

'You dared to go down that pot-hole!' she gasped. 'Oh, you naughty, plucky boys! Oh, I can't believe all this, I really can't.'

Mrs MacLaren came home at that moment, and the children streamed to meet her, shouting their news. Mrs MacLaren went pale when she heard how Sandy and Tom had actually climbed down the dangerous pot-hole.

'Well, you certainly won't do *that* again!' she said firmly. 'You might have killed yourselves!'

'But, Mother, our clothes are still down there,' said Sandy. 'We'll have to get them.'

'You are far more important to me than your clothes,' said Mrs MacLaren. 'On no account are you to go pot-hole climbing again! And now – I think I must certainly ring up the police.'

The children clustered round the phone whilst Mrs MacLaren rang the police station. They were so excited that they couldn't keep still!

'Do sit down,' begged Miss Mitchell. 'How *can* your mother phone when you are jigging about like grasshoppers!'

Mrs MacLaren, told the sergeant what the children had discovered. When the sergeant heard that Sandy had smashed the spies' radio with a stone, he roared with laughter.

'Ah, he's a bonny lad, yon boy of yours!' he said into the phone. 'He didn't wait for us to see if that radio was really doing bad work – he smashed it himself! Well, Mrs MacLaren, I'm fine and obliged to your children for doing such good work for us. This is a serious matter, and I must get on to our headquarters now, and take my orders. I'll be along at Kidillin House in a wee while!'

Mrs MacLaren put the phone down and turned to tell the children. 'Can we go with the police, Mother? Oh do let us!' begged Sandy. 'After all, we did find out everything ourselves. And if those men have escaped, by any chance, we would have to show the police how to squeeze in through the rock where the spring gushes out.'

'Very well,' said Mrs MacLaren. 'But go and put some clothes on quickly, and then come down and eat something. You must be very hungry after all these adventures.'

'Well, so I am!' said Jeanie, in surprise. 'But I was so excited that I didn't think of it till you spoke about it, Mother.'

'I'm jolly hungry too, Aunt Jessie!' said Tom. 'Come on, Sandy, let's put on shorts and jerseys, then we'll have time for something to eat before the police come.'

The children expected to see only the constable and the sergeant – and they were immensely surprised when a large black car roared up the drive to Kidillin House, with *six* policemen inside!

'Good old police!' said Sheila, watching the men jump out of the car. 'I love our London policemen, they're so tall and kind – but these police look even taller and stronger! I guess they won't stand any nonsense from the spies!'

An inspector was with the police – a stern-looking man, with the sharpest eyes Sandy had ever seen. He beckoned to Sandy and the boy went to him proudly.

'These spies may know they have been discovered, isn't that so?' asked the policeman. 'They have only to go into their cave to see their radio smashed, and they would know that someone had guessed their secret.'

'Yes, sir,' said Sandy. 'So I suggest that half your men go in the car to the other side of the mountain, and go up the slope there – it's a pretty rough road, but the car will do it all right – and the other half come with us up *this* side. Then if the spies try to escape the other way, they will be caught.'

'Good idea,' said the inspector. He gave some sharp orders, and three of the men got into the car and roared away again. When they came to the village of Kidillin, they would take the road that led around the foot of the mountain and would then go up the other side.

'Come on,' said the inspector, and he and the children and two policemen went up the hillside. The dogs, of course, went too, madly excited. Sandy said he could quiet them at any moment, and to show that he could, he held up his finger and called 'Quiet!' At once the two dogs stopped their yelping and lay down flat. The inspector nodded.

'All right,' he said. 'Come along.'

They trooped up the mountainside. When they came fairly near the old cottage, the children had a great disappointment. The inspector forbade them to come any further!'

'These men may be dangerous,' he said. 'You will stay here till I say you may move.'

'But, please, sir,' began Sandy.

'Obey orders!' said the inspector, in a sharp voice. The children stood where they were at once, and the three men went on. The dogs stood quietly by Sandy.

It seemed ages before the children heard anything more. Then they saw one of the policemen coming down the heather towards them.

'The men are gone!' he said. 'Our men the other side didn't meet them, and we've seen no sign of them. Either they've escaped us, or they're hiding somewhere on the hill. They've left their dog though. We've captured it, and it's tied to a tree. Don't let your two go near it.'

The children looked at one another in dismay and disappointment. 'So they've escaped after all!' said Tom. 'Well, what about us showing you where their radio is? We might as well do that whilst we're here.'

So the two boys took the six policemen to the hole in the rock, where the water gushed out. Two of the men squeezed through after Sandy and Tom, who once more got soaked! But they didn't care! Adventures like this didn't happen every day!

The men looked in amazement at the 'machinery' in the cave. 'What a wonderful set,' said one of the policemen, who knew all about radios. 'My word! No wonder we've had our steamers sunk here – these spies had only to watch them passing and send a radio message to the waiting submarine. We'll catch that submarine soon, or my name isn't Jock!'

'It's a strange sort of place, this,' said the other policeman, looking round.

Sandy startled the policeman very much by suddenly clutching his arm and saying 'Sh!'

'Don't do that!' said the man, scared. 'What's up?'

'I heard something over yonder,' said Sandy, pointing to the back of the cave. 'I say – I believe the spies are hiding in the mountain itself! I'm sure I heard a voice back there!'

The policeman whistled. 'Why didn't we think of that before! Come on, then – we'll hunt them out. Do you know the way?'

'Yes,' said Sandy. 'There's another cave behind this, and then a tunnel through which a shallow stream runs, and then a great underground hall, with an odd lake shining in a separate cavern.'

'Good gracious!' said the policeman, staring at Sandy in surprise. 'Well, come on, there's no time to lose.'

They followed Sandy into the next cave. The boy lighted the way with his torch. Then they all waded up the stream in the dark rocky tunnel, and came out into the enormous underground hall.

And at the other end of the great cavern they heard the sound of footfalls, as the two spies groped about, using a torch that was almost finished.

'Give yourselves up!' shouted the first policeman, and his voice echoed round thunderously. The spies put out their light and ran, stumbling and scrambling, into the cave where the underground lake shone mysteriously. Sandy remembered that the air was bad there.

He told the policeman. They put on their own torches and groped their way to the cave of the lake. The air was so bad there that the two spies, after breathing it for a minute or two, had fallen to the ground, quite stupefied.

The policemen tied handkerchiefs round their mouths and noses, and ran in. In a moment they had dragged the two men out of the lake-cave

and whilst they were still drowsy, had quickly handcuffed them. Now they could not escape!

Sandy and Tom were dancing about in excitement. The spies were caught! Their radio was smashed! Things were too marvellous for words!

It took them some time to squeeze out of the hole in the rock, with two handcuffed men, but at last they were all out. The surprise on the inspector's face outside was comical to see!

'They were in there, sir,' said a policeman, jerking his head towards the caves. 'My word, sir, you should see inside that mountain! It's a marvellous place.'

But the inspector was more interested in the capture of the spies. Each of them was handcuffed to a policeman, and down the hill they all came, policemen, spies, children – and dogs! The big dog belonging to the men was taken over the hill by one policeman, to the car left on the road below. Mack and Paddy had barked that they would eat him up, and looked as if they would too!

'So the spy-dog had better go by car!' said the inspector, smiling for the first time.

CHAPTER 12

THE END OF THE ADVENTURE

What an exciting evening the children had, telling their mother and Miss Mitchell all that had happened! Captain MacLaren came too, on twenty-four hour's leave, for the police had phoned to him, and he felt he must go and hear what had happened.

'It's a great thing, you know, catching those two spies,' he said. 'It means we'll probably get the submarine out there that's been damaging our shipping – for we'll send out a false message, and ask it to get in a certain position to sink a ship – but our aeroplanes will be there to sink the submarine instead!'

'Could we explore the inside of the mountain again, please, Uncle?' asked Tom.

'Not unless I am with you,' said Captain MacLaren firmly. 'I promise you that when I get any good leave, and can come home for two or three weeks, or when the war is over, we'll all go down there exploring together. But you must certainly not explore any more by yourselves. Also, the winter will soon be here, and the rains and snow will swell that underground lake, and the streams, and will fill the caves and tunnels almost to their roofs. It will be too dangerous.'

'Uncle, when we *do* explore the heart of the mountain with you, we could find out if the river there *is* the beginning of the Spelter,' said Tom, eagerly. 'We could throw something into it there — and watch to see if what we throw in, comes out at the foot of the mountain where the river rushes!'

'We could,' said Captain MacLaren, 'and we will! We'll have a wonderful time together, and discover all kinds of strange things!'

'But we shall never have *quite* such an exciting time again, as we've had this last week or two,' said Sandy. 'I couldn't have done it without Tom. I'm jolly glad he and Sheila came to live with us!'

'So am I!' said Tom. 'I'm proud of my Scottish cousins, Uncle Andy!'

'And I'm proud of my English nephew and niece!' said the captain, clapping Tom on the back. He looked at them with a twinkle in his eye. 'I *did* hear that you couldn't bear one another at one time,' he said, 'and that you and the dogs were all fighting together!'

'Yes, that's true,' said Sandy, going red. 'But we're all good friends now. Mack! You like old Paddy, don't you?'

Mack and Paddy were lying down side by side. At Sandy's words Mack sat up, cocked his ears, and then licked Paddy on the nose with his red tongue!

'There you are!' said Sandy, pleased. 'That shows you what good friends they are! But I shan't lick Tom's nose to show he's *my* friend!'

Everybody laughed, and then Miss Mitchell spoke.

'I wonder what's happening to those two spies,' she said. And at that very moment the telephone rang. It was the inspector, who had called up the captain to tell him the latest news.

'One of the men is a famous spy,' he said. 'We've had our eye on him for years, and he disappeared when war broke out. We are thankful to have caught him!'

'I should think so!' said the captain. 'What a bit of luck! It's difficult to round up all these spies – they're so clever at disappearing!'

'Well, sir, they won't do any more disappearing – except into prison!' chuckled the inspector. 'And now there's another bit of news, sir – I don't know if you've heard it?'

'I've heard nothing,' said the captain. 'What's the second piece of news, inspector?'

'It's about that submarine, sir. We've spotted it – and we've damaged it so that it couldn't sink itself properly.'

'Good work!' cried the captain in joy. 'That *is* a fine bit of news!'

'We've captured the submarine,' went on the inspector, 'and we've taken all the crew prisoners.'

'What have you done with the submarine?' asked the captain, whilst all the children crowded round him in excitement, trying to guess all that was said at the other end of the telephone.

'The submarine is being towed to Port Riggy,' said the inspector, 'and if the children would like to come over and see it next week, we'll be very pleased to take them over it, to show them what they've helped to capture!'

'What does he say, what does he say?' cried Sandy. 'Quick, tell us, Father!'

'Oh, he just wants to know if you'd like to go over to Port Riggy next week, and see the submarine you helped to capture!' said the captain, smiling round at the four eager faces.

'Who said we should never have such an exciting time as we've been having!' yelled Tom, dancing round like a clumsy bear. 'Golly! Think of going over a submarine! Miss Mitchell – you'll have to give us a day's holiday next week, won't you!'

'Oh, it depends on how hard you work,' said Miss Mitchell, with a wicked twinkle in her eye.

And my goodness, how hard those four children are working now! They couldn't possibly miss going over to Port Riggy to see that submarine, could they?

Smuggler Ben

Smuggler Ben

Enid Blyton
Illustrations by Paul Fisher Johnson

BLOOMSBURY
CHILDREN'S
BOOKS

Contents

CHAPTER 1

THE COTTAGE BY THE SEA

Three children got out of a bus and looked around them in excitement. Their mother smiled to see their glowing faces.

'Well, here we are!' she said. 'How do you like it?'

'Is this the cottage we're going to live in for four weeks?' said Alec, going up to the little white gate. 'Mother! It's perfect!'

The two girls, Hilary and Frances, looked at the small square cottage, and agreed with their brother. Red roses climbed all over the cottage even to the chimneys. The thatched roof came down low over the ground floor windows, and in the thatch itself other little windows jutted out.

'I wonder which is our bedroom,' said Hilary, looking up at the roof. 'I hope that one is — because it will look out over the sea.'

'Well, let's go in and see,' said Mother. 'Help

247

with the suitcases, Alec. I hope the heavy luggage has already arrived.'

They opened the white gate of Sea Cottage and went up the little stone path. It was set with orange marigolds at each side, and hundreds of the bright red-gold flowers looked up at the children as they passed.

The cottage was very small inside. The front door opened straight on to the little sitting-room. Beyond was a tiny dark kitchen. To the left was another room, whose walls were covered with bookshelves lined with books. The children stared at them in surprise.

'The man who owns this house is someone who is interested in history,' said Mother, 'so most of these books are about long-ago days, I expect. They belong to Professor Rondel. He said that you might dip into any of the books if you liked, on condition that you put them back very carefully in the right place.'

'Well, I don't think *I* shall want to do any dipping into these books!' said Hilary.

'No – dipping in the sea will suit *you* better!' laughed Frances. 'Mother, let's see our bedrooms now.'

They went upstairs. There were three bed-rooms, one very tiny indeed. Two were at the front and one was at the back. A small one and a large one were at the front, and a much bigger one behind.

'I shall have this big one,' said Mother. 'Then if Daddy comes down there will be plenty of room for him, too. Alec, you can have the tiny room overlooking the sea. And you two girls can have the one next to it.'

'That overlooks the sea, too!' said Hilary joyfully. 'But, Mother – wouldn't *you* like a room that looks out over the sea? Yours won't.'

'I shall see the sea out of this little side window,' said Mother, going to it. 'And anyway, I shall get a wonderful view of the moors at the back. You know how I love them, especially now when the heather is out.'

The children gazed out at the moors ablaze with purple heather. It was really a lovely spot.

'Blue sea in front and purple heather behind,' said Alec. 'What can anyone want better than that?'

'Well – tea for one thing,' said Frances. 'I'm most terribly hungry. Mother, could we have something to eat before we do anything?'

'If you like,' said Mother. 'We can do the unpacking afterwards. Alec, there is a tiny village down the road there, with about two shops and a few fishermen's cottages. Go with the girls and see if you can buy something for tea.'

They chattered down the narrow wooden stairway and ran out of the front door and down the path between the marigolds. They went down the sandy road, where blue chicory blossomed by the wayside and red poppies danced.

'Isn't it heavenly!' cried Hilary. 'We're at the seaside – and the holidays are just beginning. We've never been to such a lovely little place before. It's much, much nicer than the big places we've been to. I don't want bands and piers and things. I only want the yellow sands, and big rocky cliffs, and water as blue as this.'

'I vote we go down to the beach after tea, when we've helped Mother to unpack,' said Alec. 'The tide will be going out then. It comes right up to the cliffs now. Look at it splashing high up the rocks!'

The children peered over the edge of the cliff and saw the white spray flying high. It was lovely to watch. The gulls soared above their heads, making laughing cries as they went.

'I would love to be a gull for a little while,' said Frances longingly. 'Just think how glorious it would be to glide along on the wind like that for ages and ages. Sometimes I dream I'm doing that.'

'So do I,' said Hilary. 'It's a lovely feeling. Well, come on. It's no good standing here when we're getting things for tea. I'm awfully hungry.'

'You always are,' said Alec. 'I never knew such a girl. All right – come on, Frances. We can do all the exploring we want to after tea.'

They ran off. Sand got into their shoes, but they liked it. It was all part of the seashore, and there wasn't anything at the sea that they didn't like. They felt very happy.

They came to the village – though really it could hardly be called a village. There were two shops. One was a tiny baker's, which was also the little post office. The other was a general store that sold everything from pokers to strings of sausages. It was a most fascinating shop.

'It even sells foreign stamps,' said Alec, looking at some packets in the window. 'And look – that's a fine boat. I might buy that if I've got enough money.'

Hilary went to the baker's. She bought a large crusty loaf, a big cake and some currant buns. She asked for the butter and jam at the other store. The little old lady who served her smiled at the children.

'So you've come to Sea Cottage, have you?' she said. 'Well, I hope you have a good holiday. And mind you come along to see me every day, for I sell sweets, chocolates and ice-creams, as well as all the other things you see.'

'Oooh!' said Hilary. 'Well, we'll certainly come and see you then!'

They had a look at the other little cottages in the village. Fishing nets were drying outside most of them. And one or two of them were being mended. A boy of about Alec's age was mending one. He stared at the children as they passed. They didn't know whether to smile or not.

'He looks a bit fierce, doesn't he?' said Hilary. They looked back at the boy. He did look rather fierce. He was very, very dark, and his face and hands were burnt almost black. He wore an old blue jersey and long trousers, rather ragged, which he had tied up at the ankles. He was barefooted, but beside him were big sea boots.

'I don't think I like him much,' said Frances. 'He looks rather rough.'

'Well, he won't bother *us* much,' said Alec. 'He's only a fisherboy. Anyway, if he starts to be rough, *I* shall be rough, too – and he won't like that!'

'You wouldn't be nearly as strong as that fisherboy,' said Hilary.

'Yes, I would!' said Alec at once.

'No, you wouldn't,' said Hilary. 'I bet he's got muscles like iron!'

'Shut up, you two,' said Frances. 'It's too lovely a day to quarrel. Come on – let's get back home. I want my tea.'

They sat in the garden to have their tea. Mother had brought out a table and stools, and the four of them sat there happily, eating big crusty slices of bread and butter and jam, watching

the white tops of the blue waves as they swept up the shore.

'The beach looks a bit dangerous for bathing,' said Mother. 'I'm glad you are all good swimmers. Alec, you must see that you find out what times are best for bathing. Don't let the girls go in if it's dangerous.'

'We can just wear swimming costumes, Mother, can't we?' said Alec. 'And go barefoot?'

'Well, you won't want to go barefoot on those rocky cliffs, surely!' said Mother. 'You can do as you like. But just be sensible, that's all.'

'We'll help you to unpack now,' said Hilary, getting up.

'Gracious, Hilary – you don't mean to say you've had enough tea yet?' said Alec, pretending to be surprised. 'You've only had seven pieces of bread and jam, three pieces of cake and two currant buns?'

Hilary pulled Alec's hair hard and he yelled. Then they all went indoors. Mother said she would clear away the tea when they had gone down to the beach.

In half an hour all the unpacking was done and the children were free to go down to the beach. The tide was now out quite a long way and there was plenty of golden sand to run on.

'Come on!' said Alec impatiently. 'Let's go. We won't change into swimming things now, it will waste time. We'll go as we are!'

So off they sped, down the marigold path, through the white gate, and into the sandy lane. A small path led across the grassy cliff top to where steep steps had been cut in the cliff itself in order that people might get up and down.

'Down we go!' said Alec. 'My word – doesn't the sea look grand. I've never seen it so blue in my life!'

CHAPTER 2

A HORRID BOY – AND
A DISAPPOINTMENT

They reached the beach. It was wet from the tide and gleamed brightly as they walked on it. Their feet made little prints on it that faded almost as soon as they were made. Gleaming shells lay here and there, as pink as sunset.

There were big rocks sticking up everywhere, and around them were deep and shallow pools. The children loved paddling in them because they were so warm. They ran down to the edge of the sea and let the white edges of the waves curl over their toes. It was all lovely.

'The fishing boats are out,' said Alec, shading his eyes as he saw the boats setting out on the tide, their white sails gleaming in the sun. 'And listen – is that a motorboat?'

It was. One came shooting by at a great pace, and then another. They came from the big

seaside town not far off where many trippers
went. The children watched them fly past, the
white spray flying into the air.

They wandered along by the sea, exploring all
the rock pools, picking up shells and splashing
in the edge of the water. They saw nobody at all
until they rounded a rocky corner of the beach
and came to a small cove, well hidden between
two jutting-out arms of the cliff.

They heard the sound of whistling, and
stopped. Sitting beside a small boat, doing
something to it, was the fisherboy they had seen
before tea.

He now had on his sea boots, a red fisherman's
cap with a tassel hanging down, and a bright red
scarf tied round his trousers.

'That's the same boy we saw before,' said Alec.

The boy heard the sound of voices on the
breeze and looked up. He scowled, and his dark
face looked savage. He stood up and looked
threateningly towards the three children.

'Well, he looks fiercer than ever,' said Hilary,
at last. 'What's the matter with him, I wonder?
He doesn't look at all pleased to see us.'

'Let's go on and take no notice of him,' said
Alec. 'He's no right to glare at us like that.
We're doing no harm!'

So the three children walked into the hidden
cove, not looking at the fisherboy at all. But as

soon as they had taken three or four steps, the boy shouted at them loudly.

'Hey, you there! Keep out of this cove!'

The children stopped. 'Why should we?' said Alec.

'Because it belongs to me,' said the boy. 'You keep out of this. It's been my cove for years, and no one's come here. I won't have you trippers coming into it and spoiling it.'

'We're *not* trippers!' cried Hilary indignantly. 'We're staying at Sea Cottage for a whole month.'

'Well, you're trippers for a month then instead of for a day!' said the boy sulkily. 'Clear off! I tell you. This is my own place here. I don't want anyone else in it. If you come here I'll set on you and beat you off.'

The boy really looked so fierce that the children felt quite frightened. Then out of his belt he took a gleaming knife. That settled things for the two girls. They weren't going to have any quarrel with a savage boy who held such a sharp knife.

But Alec was furious. 'How dare you threaten us with a knife!' he shouted. 'You're a coward. I haven't a knife or I'd fight you.'

'Alec! Come away!' begged Frances, clutching hold of her brother. 'Do come away. I think that boy's mad. He looks it anyway.'

The boy stood watching them, feeling the sharp edge of his knife with his thumb. His sullen face looked as black as thunder.

Frances and Hilary dragged Alec off round the rocky corner. He struggled with them to get free, and they tore his flannel shirt.

'Now look what you've done!' he cried angrily. 'Let me go!'

'Alec, it's seven o'clock already and Mother said we were to be back by then,' said Hilary, looking at her watch. 'Let's go back. We can settle with that horrid boy another day.'

Alec shook himself free and set off home with the girls rather sulkily. He felt that the evening had been spoilt. It had all been so lovely – and now that nasty boy had spoilt everything.

The girls told their mother about the boy, and she was astonished. 'Well, he certainly does sound rather mad,' she said. 'For goodness' sake don't start quarrelling with him. Leave him alone.'

'But, Mother, if he won't let us go into the little coves, it's not fair,' said Hilary.

Mother laughed. 'Don't worry about that!' she said. 'There will be plenty of times when he's busy elsewhere, and the places you want to go to will be empty. Sometimes the people who live in a place do resent others coming to stay in it for a while.'

'Mother, could we have a boat, do you think?' asked Alec. 'It would be such fun.'

'I'll go and see about one for you tomorrow,' said Mother. 'Now it's time you all went to bed. Hilary is yawning so widely that I can almost count her teeth!'

They were all tired. They fell into bed and went to sleep at once, although Hilary badly wanted to lie awake for a time and listen to the lovely noise the sea made outside her window. But she simply couldn't keep her eyes open, and in about half a minute she was as sound asleep as the other two.

It was lovely to wake up in the morning and remember everything. Frances woke first and sat up. She saw the blue sea shining in the distance and she gave Hilary a sharp dig.

'Hilary! Wake up! We're at the seaside!'

Hilary woke with a jump. She sat up, too, and gazed out to the sea, over which white gulls were soaring. She felt so happy that she could hardly speak. Then Alec appeared at the door in his swimming trunks. He had nothing else on at all, and his face was excited.

'I'm going for a dip,' he said in a low voice. 'Are you coming? Don't wake Mother. It's early.'

The girls almost fell out of bed in their excitement. They pulled on swimming costumes, and then crept out of the cottage with Alec.

It was about half-past six. The world looked clean and new. 'Just as if it has been freshly washed,' said Hilary, sniffing the sharp, salt breeze. 'Look at those pink clouds over there! And did you ever see such a clear blue as the sea is this morning. Ooooh – it's cold!'

It *was* cold. The children ran into the water a little way and then stopped and shivered. Alec plunged right under and came up, shaking the drops from his hair. 'Come on!' he yelled. 'It's gorgeous once you're in!'

The girls were soon right under, and the three of them spent twenty minutes swimming out and back, diving under the water and catching each other's legs, then floating happily on their backs, looking up into the clear morning sky.

'Time to come out,' said Alec, at last. 'Come on. Race you up the cliff!'

But they had to go slowly up the cliff, for the steps really were very steep. They burst into the cottage to find Mother up and bustling round to get breakfast ready.

At half-past seven they were all having breakfast. Afterwards Mother said she would tidy round the house and then do the shopping. The girls and Alec must make their own beds, just as they did at home.

'When we are down in the village I'll make enquiries about a boat for you,' promised

Mother, when at last the beds were made, the kitchen and sitting-room tidied and set in order. 'Now, are we ready? Bring that big basket, Alec. I shall want that.'

'Mother, we must buy spades,' said Alec. 'That sand would be gorgeous to dig in.'

'Gracious! Aren't you too big to dig?' said Mother. The children laughed.

'Mother, you're not too big either! Don't you remember how you helped us to dig that simply enormous castle last year, with the big moat round it? It had steps all the way up it and was simply lovely.'

They set off joyously, Alec swinging the basket. They did a lot of shopping at the little general store, and the little old lady beamed at them.

'Do you know where I can arrange about hiring a boat for my children?' Mother asked her.

'Well,' said the old lady, whose name was Mrs Polsett, 'I really don't know. We use all our boats hereabouts, you know. You could ask Samuel. He lives in the cottage over yonder. He's got a small boat as well as a fishing boat. Maybe he'd let the children have it.'

So Mother went across to where Samuel was sitting mending a great fishing net. He was an old man with bright blue eyes and a wrinkled face like a shrivelled brown apple.

'Have you a boat I could hire for my children?' Mother asked.

Samuel shook his head. 'No,' he said. 'I have got one, it's true – but I'm not hiring it out any more. Some boys had it last year, and they lost the oars and made a great hole in the bottom. I lost more money on that there boat than I made.'

'Well, I'm sure my three children would be very careful indeed,' said Mother, seeing the disappointed faces around her. 'Won't you lend it to them for a week and see how they get on? I will pay you well.'

'No, thank you kindly,' said Samuel firmly.

'Is there anyone else who has a boat to spare?' said Alec, feeling rather desperate, for he had really set his heart on a boat.

'No one that I know of,' said Samuel. 'Some of us lost our small boats in a big storm this year, when the sea came right over the cliffs, the waves were so big. Maybe I'll take the children out in my fishing boat if they're well behaved.'

'Thank you,' said Hilary. But they all looked very disappointed, because going out in somebody else's boat wasn't a bit the same as having their own.

'We'll just go back to old Mrs Polsett's shop and see if she knows of anyone else with a boat,' said Mother. So back they went.

But the old lady shook her head.

'The only other person who has a boat – and it's not much of a boat, all patched and mended,' she said, 'is Smuggler Ben.'

'Smuggler Ben!' said Alec. 'Is there a smuggler here? Where does he live?'

'Oh, he's not a real smuggler!' said Mrs Polsett, with a laugh. 'He's my grandson. But he's just mad on tales of the old-time smugglers, and he likes to pretend he's one. There were smugglers' caves here, you know, somewhere about the beach. I dare say Ben knows them. Nobody else does now.'

The children felt terribly excited. Smugglers – and caves! And who was Smuggler Ben? They felt that they would very much like to know him. And he had a boat, too. He would be a fine person to know!

'Is Smuggler Ben grown-up?' asked Alec.

'Bless you, no!' said Mrs Polsett. 'He's much the same age as you. Look – there he goes – down the street there!'

The children turned to look. And as soon as they saw the boy, their hearts sank.

'It's the nasty boy with the knife!' said Hilary sadly. '*He* won't lend us his boat.'

'Don't you worry about his knife,' said old Mrs Polsett. 'It's all pretence with him. He's just play-acting most of the time. He always wishes he could have been a smuggler, and he's for ever pretending he is one. There's no harm in him. He's a good boy for work – and when he wants to play, well, let him play as he likes, I say! He doesn't get into mischief like most boys do. He goes off exploring the cliffs, and rows in his boat half the time. But he does keep himself to himself. Shall I ask him if he'll lend you his boat sometimes?'

'No, thank you,' said Alec politely. He was sure the boy would refuse rudely, and Alec wasn't going to give him the chance to do that.

They walked back to Sea Cottage. They felt sad about the boat – but their spirits rose as they saw their swimming costumes lying on the grass, bone-dry.

'What about another swim before lunch?' cried Alec. 'Come on, Mother. You must come, too!'

So down to the sea they all went again, and by the squeals, shrieks and shouts, four people had a really wonderful time!

CHAPTER 3

HILARY HAS AN ADVENTURE

One evening, after tea, Frances and Alec wanted to go for a long walk. 'Coming, Hilary?' they said. Hilary shook her head.

'No,' she said. 'I'm a bit tired with all my swimming today. I'll take a book and go and sit on the cliff top till you come back.'

So Alec went off with Frances, and Hilary took her book and went to find a nice place to sit. She could see miles and miles of restless blue sea from the cliff. It was really marvellous. She walked on the cliff edge towards the east, found a big gorse bush and sat down beside it for shelter. She opened her book.

When she looked up, something nearby caught her eye. It looked like a little-worn path going straight to the cliff edge. 'A rabbit path, I suppose,' said Hilary to herself. 'But fancy the rabbits going right over the steep cliff edge like

267

that! I suppose there must be a hole there that they pop into.'

She got up to look – and to her great surprise saw what looked like a narrow, rocky path going down the cliff side, very steep indeed! In a sandy ledge a little way down was the print of a bare foot.

'Well, *someone* has plainly gone down this steep path!' thought Hilary. 'I wonder who it was. I wonder where it leads to. I've a good mind to find out!'

She began to go down the path. It really was very steep and rather dangerous. At one extremely dangerous part someone had driven in iron bars and stretched a piece of strong rope from bar to bar. Hilary was glad to get hold of it, for her feet were sliding down by themselves and she was afraid she was going to fall.

When she was about three-quarters of the way down she heard the sound of someone whistling very quietly. She stopped and tried to peer down to see who was on the beach.

'Why, this path leads down to that little cove we saw the other day!' she thought excitedly. 'The one where the rude boy was. Oh, I hope he isn't there now!'

He was! He was sitting on his upturned boat, whittling at something with his sharp knife. Hilary turned rather pale when she saw the knife. It was all very well for old Mrs Polsett to say that her grandson was only play-acting – but Hilary was sure that Ben really felt himself to be somebody fierce – and he might act like that, too.

As she stood and watched him, unseen, she saw the sharp knife slip. The boy gave a cry of pain and clutched his left hand. He had cut it very badly indeed. Blood began to drip on to the sand.

The boy felt in his pocket for something to bind up his hand. But he could find nothing. He pressed the cut together, but it went on bleeding. Hilary was tender-hearted and she couldn't bear to see the boy's face all screwed up in pain, and do nothing about it.

She forgot to be afraid of him. She went down the last piece of cliff and jumped down on the sand. The boy heard her and turned, his face one big scowl. Hilary ran up to him.

She had a big clean handkerchief in her pocket, and she took this out. 'I'll tie up your hand for you,' she said. 'I say – what an *awful* cut! I should howl like anything if I did that to myself.'

The boy scowled at her again. 'What are you doing here?' he said. 'Where are the others?'

'I'm alone,' said Hilary. 'I found that funny steep path and came down it to see where it led to. And I saw you cut your hand. Give it to me. Come on, Ben – hold it out and let me tie it up. You might bleed to death if you go on like this.'

The boy held out his cut hand. 'How do you know my name is Ben?' he said in a surly voice.

'Never mind how I know!' said Hilary. 'You're Smuggler Ben! What a marvellous name! Don't you wish you really *were* a smuggler? I do! I'm just reading a book about smuggling and it's terribly exciting.'

'What book?' asked the boy.

Hilary bound up his hand well, and then showed him the book. 'It's all about hidden caves and smugglers coming in at night and things like that,' she said. 'I'll lend it to you if you like.'

The boy stared at her. He couldn't help liking this little girl with her honest eyes and clear, kind little voice. His hand felt much more comfortable now, too. He was grateful to her. He took the book and looked through the pages.

'I'd like to read it after you,' he said more graciously. 'I can't get enough books. Do you really like smuggling and that kind of thing?'

'Of course,' said Hilary. 'I like anything adventurous like that. Is it true that there are smugglers' caves along this coast somewhere?'

The boy stopped before he answered. 'If I tell you, will you keep it a secret?' he said, at last.

'Well – I could tell the others, couldn't I?'

said Hilary. 'We all share everything, you know, Alec and Frances and I.'

'No, I don't want you to tell anyone,' said the boy. 'It's my own secret. I wouldn't mind sharing it with you, because you've helped me, and you like smuggling, too. But I don't want the others to know.'

'Then don't tell me,' said Hilary, disappointed. 'You see, it would be mean of me to keep an exciting thing like that from the others. I just couldn't do it. You'd know how I feel if you had brothers and sisters. You just have to share exciting things.'

'I haven't got any brothers or sisters,' said the boy. 'I wish I had. I always play alone. There aren't any boys of my age in our village – only girls, and I don't like girls. They're silly.'

'Oh well, if you think that, I'll go,' said Hilary, offended. She turned to go, but the boy caught her arm.

'No, don't go. I didn't mean that *you* were silly. I don't think you are. I think you're sensible. Let me tell you one of my secrets.'

'Not unless I can share it with the others,' said Hilary. 'I'm simply longing to know – but I don't want to leave the others out of it.'

'Are they as sensible as you are?' asked Ben.

'Of course,' said Hilary. 'As a matter of fact, Frances, my sister, is nicer than I am. I'm always losing my temper and she doesn't. You can trust us, Ben, really you can.'

'Well,' said Ben slowly, 'I'll let you all into my secret then. I'll show you something that will make you stare! Come here tomorrow, down that little path. I'll be here, and just see if I don't astonish you.'

Hilary's eyes shone. She felt excited. She caught hold of Ben's arm and looked at him eagerly.

'You're a sport!' she said. 'I like you, Smuggler Ben. Let's all be smugglers, shall we?'

Ben smiled for the first time. His brown face changed completely, and his dark eyes twinkled. 'All right,' he said. 'We'll all be. That would be more fun than playing alone, if I can trust you all not to say a word to any grown-up. They might interfere. And now I'll tell you one little secret – and you can tell the others if you like. I know where the old smugglers' caves are!'

'Ben!' cried Hilary, her eyes shining with excitement. 'Do you really? I wondered if you did. Oh, I say, isn't that simply marvellous! Will you show us them tomorrow? Oh, do say you will.'

'You wait and see,' said Ben. He turned his boat the right way up and dragged it down the beach.

'Where are you going?' called Hilary.

'Back home in my boat,' said Ben. 'I've got to go out fishing with my uncle tonight. Would you like to come back in my boat with me? It'll save you climbing up that steep path.'

'Oh, I'd love to!' said Hilary joyfully. 'You know, Ben, we tried and tried to hire a boat of our own, but we couldn't. We were so terribly disappointed. Can I get in? You push her out.'

Ben pushed the boat out on to the waves and then got in himself. But when he took the oars he found that his cut hand was far too painful to handle the left oar. He bit his lip and went a little pale under his tan.

'What's the matter?' said Hilary. 'Oh, it's your hand. Well, let me take the oars. I can row. Yes, I can, Ben! You'll only make your cut bleed again.'

Ben gave up his seat and the girl took the oars. She rowed very well indeed, and the oars cut cleanly into the water. The boat flew along over the waves.

'You don't row badly for a girl,' said Ben.

'Well, we live near a river at home,' said Hilary, 'and we are often out in our uncle's boat. We can all row. So you can guess how disappointed we were when we found that we couldn't get a boat here for ourselves.'

Ben was silent for a little while. Then he spoke again. 'Well – I don't mind lending you my boat sometimes, if you like. When I'm out

fishing, you can have it — but don't you dare to spoil it in any way. I know it's only an old boat, but I love it.'

Hilary stopped rowing and looked at Ben in delight. 'I say, you really are a brick!' she said. 'Do you mean it?'

'I always mean what I say,' said Ben gruffly. 'You lend me your books — and I'll lend you my boat.'

Hilary rowed all round the cliffs until she came to the beach she knew. She rowed inshore and they got out. She and Ben pulled the boat right up the beach and turned it upside down.

'I must go now,' said Ben. 'My uncle's waiting for me. See you tomorrow.'

He went off, and Hilary turned to go home. At the top of the beach she saw Frances and Alec staring at her in amazement.

'Hilary! Were you with that awful boy in his boat?' cried Frances. 'However did you dare?'

'He isn't awful after all,' said Hilary. 'He's quite nice. He's got wonderful secrets — simply wonderful. And he says we can use his boat when he doesn't want it!'

The other two stared open-mouthed. They simply couldn't believe all this. Why, that boy had threatened them with a knife — he couldn't possibly be nice enough to lend them his boat.

'I'll tell you all about it,' said Hilary, as they

set off up the cliff path. 'You see, I found a little secret way down to that cove we saw – and Ben was there.'

She told them the whole story and they listened in silence.

'Things always happen to you, Hilary,' said Frances rather enviously. 'Well, I must say this is all very exciting. I can hardly wait till tomorrow. Do you really think Smuggler Ben will show us those caves? I wonder where they are? I hope they aren't miles away!'

'Well, we'll see,' said Hilary happily. They went home hungry to their supper – and in bed that night each of them dreamt of caves and smugglers and all kinds of exciting things. This holiday promised to be more thrilling than they had imagined.

CHAPTER 4

AN EXCITING EVENING

The children told their mother about Ben. She was amused.

'So the fierce little boy has turned out to be quite ordinary after all!' she said. 'Well, I must say I'm glad. I didn't very much like to think of a little savage rushing about the shore armed with a sharp knife. I think it's very nice of him to lend you his boat. You had better bring him in to a meal, and then I can see him for myself.'

'Oh, thanks, Mother,' said Hilary. 'I say – do you think we could get ourselves some fishermen's hats, like Ben wears – and have you got a bright-coloured scarf or sash that you could lend us, Mother? Or three, if you've got them. We're going to play smugglers, and it would be fun to dress up a bit. Ben does. He looks awfully grand in his tasselled hat and sash and big boots.'

'Hilary, you don't seriously think I am going

to hand you out all my precious scarves, do you?' said Mother. 'I'll give you some money to go and buy three cheap hats and scarves with, if you like – and you can all wear your wellingtons if you want big boots. But I draw the line at getting you sharp knives like Ben. Look how even he cut himself today!'

The children were delighted to think they could buy something they could dress up in. The next morning they set off to Mrs Polsett's and asked to see fishermen's hats. She had a few and brought them out. 'I knitted them myself,' she said. 'Here's a red one with a yellow tassel. That would suit you fine, Hilary.'

So it did. Hilary pulled it on and swung the tasselled end over her left ear just as she had seen Ben do.

Frances chose a blue one with a red tassel and Alec chose a green one with a brown tassel. Then they bought some very cheap scarves to tie round their waists.

They went back home, pulled on their wellingtons, and put on their hats and sashes.

They looked grand.

Hilary showed them where the little narrow path ran down the steep cliff.

'Goodness,' said Alec, peering over the edge. 'What a terrifying way down! I feel half-afraid of falling. I'm sure I can never get down those steep bits.'

'There's a rope tied there,' said Hilary, going down first. 'Come on. Ben will be waiting. I saw his boat out on the water as we came along the cliff.'

They all went down the path slowly for fear of falling. When they jumped down the last rocky step into the little cove, they saw Ben there waiting for them, sitting on his little boat. He was dressed just as they were, except that his boots were real sea boots, and he wore trousers tucked well down into them. He didn't move as they came up, nor did he smile.

'Hello, Ben!' said Hilary. 'I've brought my brother and sister as you said I could. This is Alec, and this is Frances. I've told them what you said. We're all terribly excited.'

'Did you tell them it's all a deep secret?' said Ben, looking at Hilary. 'They won't give it away?'

'Of course we won't,' said Alec indignantly. 'That would spoil all the fun. I say – can we call you Smuggler Ben? It sounds fine.'

Ben looked pleased. Yes, you can,' he said. 'And remember, I'm the captain. You've got to obey my orders.'

'Oh,' said Alec, not liking this idea quite so much. 'Well – all right. Lead on. Show us your secret.'

'You know, don't you, that there really were

smugglers here in the old days?' said Ben. 'They came up the coast quietly on dark nights, bringing in all kinds of goods. Folk here knew they came, but they were afraid of them. They used to take the goods to the old caves here, and hide them there till they could get rid of them overland.'

'And do you really know where the caves are?' said Alec eagerly. 'My word, Smuggler Ben – you're a wonder!'

Smuggler Ben smiled and his brown face changed at once. 'Come on,' he said. 'I'll show you something that will surprise you!'

He led the way up the beach to the cliffs at the back. 'Now,' he said, 'the entrance to the old caves is somewhere in this little cove. Before I show you, see if you can find it!'

'In the cove!' cried Hilary. 'Oh, I guess we shall soon find it then!'

The three children began to hunt carefully along the rocky cliff. They ran into narrow caves and out again. They came to a big cave, went into that and came out again. It seemed nothing but a large cave, narrowing at the back. There were no more caves after that one, and the children turned in disappointment to Ben.

'You don't mean that these little caves and that one big one are the old smuggling caves do you?' said Hilary. 'Because they are just like heaps of other caves we have seen at the seaside.'

'No, I don't mean that,' said Ben. 'Now, you come with me and I'll show you something exciting.'

He led them into the big cave. He took them to the right of it and then jumped up to a rocky ledge which was just about shoulder high. In half a moment he had completely disappeared! Hilary felt about up the ledge and called to him in bewilderment.

'Ben! Smuggler Ben! Where have you gone?'

There was no answer. The three children stared up at the ledge. Alec jumped up to it. He felt all along it, up and down and sideways. He simply couldn't imagine where Ben had gone to!

There was a low laugh behind them. The children turned in surprise – and there was Ben, standing at the entrance to the big cave, laughing all over his brown face at their surprise.

'Ben! What happened? Where did you disappear to? And how did you get back to the entrance without us seeing you?' cried Hilary. 'It's like magic. Do tell us. Quick!'

'Well, I'll show you,' said Ben. 'I found it out quite by accident. One day I came into this cave and fell asleep. When I woke up, the tide was high and was already coming into the cave. I was trapped. I couldn't possibly get out, because I knew I'd be dashed against the rocks outside, the sea was so stormy.'

'So you climbed up on to this ledge!' cried Hilary.

'Yes, I did,' said Ben. 'It was the only thing to do. I just hoped and hoped the sea wouldn't fill the cave up completely, or I knew I'd be drowned. Well, I crouched there for ages, the sea getting higher and higher up till it reached the ledge.'

'Gracious!' said Frances, shivering. 'You must have been afraid.'

'I was, rather,' said Ben. 'Well, I rolled right to the back of the ledge, and put up my hand to catch hold of any bit of jutting-out rock that I could – and instead of knocking against rock, my hand went into space!'

'What do you mean?' said Alec in astonishment.

'Come and see,' said Ben, and he took a torch out of his pocket. All the children climbed on to the ledge, and squeezed together there, watching the beam of Ben's torch. He directed it upwards – and then, to their amazement, they saw a perfectly round hole going upwards right at the far corner of the rocky ledge. It didn't look very big.

'See that?' said Ben. 'Well, when I felt my hand going up that hole I slid over to this corner and put my arm right up the hole. And this is what I found.'

He shone his torch up the rounded hole in the

rock. The three children peered up, one after another.

Driven into the rock were great thick nails, one above the other. 'See those?' said Ben. 'Well, I reckon they were put there by some old-time smuggler.'

'Did you get up the hole?' asked Alec.

'You bet I did!' said Ben. 'And pretty quick, too, for the sea was washing inches above the ledge by that time and I was soaked through. I squeezed myself up, got my feet on those nails – they're sort of steps up, you see – and climbed up the hole by feeling for the nails with my feet.'

'Where does the hole lead to?' asked Frances in excitement.

'You'd better come and see,' said Ben, with a sudden grin. The children asked nothing better than that, and at once Alec put his head up the hole. It was not such a tight fit as he expected. He was easily able to climb up. There were about twenty nails for footholds and then they stopped. There was another ledge to climb out on. The boy dragged himself there, and looked down.

'Can't see a thing!' he called. 'Come on up, Smuggler Ben, and bring your torch.'

'I'll give Hilary my torch,' said Ben. 'She can shine it for you up there when she's up, and shine it down for us to climb up by, too. Go on, Hilary.'

So Hilary went up next with the torch – and when she shone it around her at the top, she and Alec gave a shout of astonishment.

They were on a ledge near the ceiling of a most enormous cave. It looked almost as big as a church to the children. The floor was of rock, not of sand. Strange lights shone in the walls. They came from the twinkling bits of metal in the rocks.

'Frances! Hurry,' cried Hilary. 'It's marvellous here.'

Soon all four children were standing on the ledge, looking down into the great cave. In it, on the floor, were many boxes of all kinds – small, big, square, oblong. Bits of rope were scattered about, too, and an old broken lantern lay in a corner.

'*Real* smugglers have been here!' said Hilary in a whisper.

'What are you whispering for?' said Alec with a laugh. 'Afraid they will hear you?'

'No – but it all seems so mysterious,' said Hilary. 'Let's get down to the floor of the cave. How do we get there?'

'Jump,' said Ben.

So they jumped. They ran to the boxes and opened the lids.

'No good,' said Ben. 'I've done that long ago. They're quite empty. I often come to play

smugglers here when I'm by myself. Isn't it a fine place?'

'Simply marvellous!' said Alec. 'Let's all come here and play tomorrow. We can bring candles and something to eat and drink. It would be gorgeous.'

'Oooh, yes,' said Hilary. So they planned everything in excitement, and then climbed back to the ledge, and down through the hole into the first cave. Out they went into the sunshine. Ben smiled as much as the rest.

'It's fun to share my secret with you,' he told the others half-shyly. 'It will be grand to play smugglers all together, instead of just by myself. I'll bring some sandwiches tomorrow, and some plums. You bring anything you can, too. It shall be our own secret smugglers' cave — and we're the smugglers!'

CHAPTER 5

YET ANOTHER SECRET

The next day the four children met together in the big cave. They felt very thrilled as they climbed up the hole and then jumped down into the smugglers' cave. They had brought candles and food with them, and Alec had bottles of home-made lemonade on his back in a leather bag.

They played smugglers to their hearts' content. Ben ordered them about, and called them 'My men', and everyone enjoyed the game thoroughly. At last, Alec sat down on a big box and said he was tired of playing.

'I'd like something to eat,' he said. 'Let's use this big box for a table.'

They set the things out on the table. And then Hilary looked in a puzzled way at the box.

'What's up?' asked Alec, seeing her look.

'Well, I'm just wondering something,' said

287

Hilary. 'How in the world did the smugglers get this big box up the small round hole to this cave? After all, that hole only just takes us comfortably – surely this box would never have got through it.'

Frances and Alec stared at the box. They felt puzzled, too. It was quite certain that no one could have carried such a big box through the hole. They looked at Ben.

'Have you ever thought of that?' Alec asked him.

'Plenty of times,' said Ben. 'And, what's more, I know the answer!'

'Tell us!' begged Hilary. 'Is there another way into this cave?'

Smuggler Ben nodded. 'Yes,' he said. 'I'll show it to you if you like. I just wanted to see if any of my three men were clever enough to think of such a thing. Come on – I'll show you the other way in. Didn't you wonder yesterday how it was that I came back into the other cave after I'd disappeared up the hole?'

He stood up and the others rose, too, all excited. Ben went to the back of the cave. It seemed to the children as if the wall there was quite continuous – but it wasn't. There was a fold in it – and in the fold was a passage! It was wide, but low, and the children had to crouch down almost double to get into it. But almost immediately it rose high and they could stand. Smuggler Ben switched on his torch, and the children saw that the passage was quite short and led into yet another cave. This was small and ran right down to the rocky side of the cliff very steeply, more like a wide passage than a cave.

The children went down the long cave and came to a rocky inlet of water. 'When the tide comes in, it sweeps right through this cave,' said Ben, 'and I reckon that this is where the smugglers brought in their goods – by boat. The boat would be guided into this watery passage at high tide, and beached at the far end, where the tide didn't reach. Then the things could easily be taken into the big cave. The smugglers left a way of escape for themselves down the hole we climbed through from the first cave – you know, where the nails are driven into the rock.'

'This gets more and more exciting!' said Alec. 'Anything more, Ben? Don't keep it from us. Tell us everything!'

'Well, there is one thing more,' said Ben, 'but it just beats me. Maybe the four of us together could do something about it, though. Come along and I'll show you.'

He led them back to the little passage between the big cave and the one they were in. He climbed up the wall a little way and then disappeared. The others followed him.

There was another passage leading off into the darkness there, back into the cliff. Ben shone his torch down it as the others crowded on his heels.

'Let's go up it!' cried Alec excitedly.

'We can't,' said Ben, and he shone his torch before him. 'The passage walls have fallen in just along there – look!'

So they had. The passage ended in a heap of stones, soil and sand. It was completely blocked up.

'Can't we clear it?' cried Alec.

'Well, we might, as there are so many of us,' said Ben. 'I didn't feel like tackling it all by myself, I must say. For one thing I didn't know how far back the passage was blocked. It might have fallen in for a long way.'

'I wonder where it leads to,' said Alec. 'It seems to go straight back. I say – isn't this thrilling!'

'We'll come and dig it out tomorrow,' said Hilary, her eyes dancing. 'We'll bring our spades – and a sack or something to put the stones and soil in. Then we can drag it away and empty it.'

'Be here tomorrow after tea,' said Smuggler Ben, laughing. 'I'll bring my uncle's big spade. That's a powerful one – it will soon dig away the soil.'

So the next day the children crowded into the cave with spades and sacks. They used the ordinary way in, climbing up the hole by the nails and jumping into the cave from the high ledge. Then they made their way into the low passage, and climbed up where the roof rose high, till they came to the blocked-up passage. They went on by the light of their torches and came to the big fall of stones and soil.

'Now, men, to work!' said Smuggler Ben, and the gang set to work with a will. The boys shovelled away the soil and stones, and the girls filled the sacks. Then the boys dragged them down the passage, let them fall into the opening between the two caves, climbed down, dragged the sacks into the large cave and emptied them into a corner. Then back they went again to do some more digging.

'What's the time?' said Alec, at last. 'I feel as if we've been working for hours. We mustn't forget that high tide is at half-past seven. We've got to get out before then.'

Hilary looked at her watch. 'It's all right,' she said. 'It's only half-past six. We've plenty of time.'

'Gracious! Hasn't the time gone slowly!' said Frances in surprise. 'Come on – we can do a lot more!'

They went on working, and after a time Ben began to feel rather uncomfortable. 'Hilary, what's the time now?' he said. 'I'm sure it must be getting near high tide.'

Hilary glanced at her watch again. 'It's half-past six,' she said in surprise.

'But you said that before!' cried Ben. 'Has your watch stopped?'

It had! Hilary held it to her ear and cried out in dismay. 'Yes! It's stopped. Oh blow! I wonder what the right time is.'

'Quick! We'd better go and see how the tide is,' said Ben, and he dropped his spade and rushed to the entrance of the blocked-up passage. He dropped down and went into the big cave, and then climbed up to the ledge, and then down by the nail studded hole on to the ledge in the first cave.

But even as he climbed down to the ledge, he felt the wash of water over his foot. 'Gosh! The tide's almost in!' he yelled. 'We're caught! We can't get out!'

He climbed back and stood in the big cave with the others. They looked at him, half-frightened.

'Don't be scared,' said Smuggler Ben. 'It only means we'll have to wait a few hours till the tide goes down. I hope your mother won't worry.'

'She's out tonight,' said Alec. 'She won't know. Does the water come in here, Ben?'

'Of course not,' said Ben. 'This cave is too high up. Well – let's sit down, have some chocolate and a rest, and then, we might as well get on with our job.'

Time went on. The boys went to see if the tide was falling, but it was still very high. It was getting dark outside. The boys stood at the end of the long, narrow cave, up which the sea now rushed deeply. And as they stood there, they heard a strange noise coming nearer and nearer.

'Whatever's that?' said Alec in astonishment.

'It sounds like a motorboat,' said Ben.

'It can't be,' said Alec.

But it was. A small motorboat suddenly loomed out of the darkness and worked itself very carefully up the narrow passage and into the long cave, which was now full of deep water! The boys were at first too startled to move. They heard men and women talking in low voices.

'Is this the place?'

'Yes – step out just there. Wait till the wave goes back. That's it – now step out.'

Ben clutched hold of Alec's arm and pulled him silently away, back into the entrance between the caves. Up they went in the blocked passage. The girls called out to them: 'What's the tide like?'

'Sh!' said Smuggler Ben, so fiercely that the girls were quite frightened. They stared at Ben with big eyes. The boy told them in a whisper what he and Alec had seen.

'Something's going on,' he said mysteriously. 'I don't know what. But it makes me suspicious

when strange motorboats come to our coasts late
at night like this and run into a little-known
cave. After all, our country is at war – they may

be up to no good, these people. They may be
enemies!'

All the children felt a shivery feeling down
their backs when Ben said this. Hilary felt that it
was just a bit *too* exciting. 'What do you mean?'
she whispered.

'I don't exactly know,' said Ben. 'All I know
for certain is that it's plain somebody else knows
of these caves and plans to use them for something. I don't know what. And it's up to us to
find out!'

'Oooh! I wish we could!' said Hilary, at once.
'What are we going to do now? Wait here?'

'Alec and I will go down to the beginning of
this passage,' said Ben. 'Maybe the people don't
know about it. We'll see if we can hear what they
say.'

So they crept down to the beginning of the
passage and leaned over to listen. Three or four
people had now gone into the big cave, but to
Ben's great disappointment they were talking in
a strange language, and he could not understand
a word.

Then came something he *did* understand! One
of the women spoke in English. 'We will bring
them on Thursday night,' she said. 'When the
tide is full.'

Another man answered. Then the people went
back to their motorboat, and the boys soon heard

the whirring of the engine as it made its way carefully out of the long, narrow cave.

'They're using that cave rather like a boathouse,' said Ben. 'Golly, I wonder how they knew about it. And what are they bringing in on Thursday night?'

'Smuggled goods, do you think?' said Alec, hot with excitement. 'People always smuggle things in wartime. Mother said so. They're smugglers, Ben – smugglers of nowadays! And they're using the old smugglers' caves again. I say – isn't this awfully exciting?'

'Yes, it is,' said Smuggler Ben. 'We'd better come here on Thursday night, Alec. We'll have to see what happens. We simply must. Can you slip away at about midnight, do you think?'

'Of course!' said Alec. 'You bet! And the girls, too! We'll all be here! And we'll watch to see exactly what happens. Fancy spying on real smugglers, Ben. What a thrill!'

CHAPTER 6

A STRANGE DISCOVERY

Mother was in by the time the children got back home, and she was very worried indeed about them.

'Mother, it's all right,' said Alec, going over to her. 'We just got caught by the tide, that's all, playing in caves. But we were quite safe. We just waited till the tide went down.'

'Now listen, Alec,' said Mother, 'this just won't do. I shall forbid you to play in those caves if you get caught another time and worry me like this. I imagined you all drowning or something.'

'We're awfully sorry, Mother,' said Hilary, putting her arms round her. 'Really, we wouldn't have worried you for anything. Look – my watch stopped at half-past six, and that put us all wrong about the tide.'

'Very well,' said Mother. 'I'll forgive you this

time – but I warn you, if you worry me again like this you won't be allowed to set foot in a single cave!'

The next day it poured with rain, which was very disappointing. Alec ran down to the village to see what Ben was doing. The two girls talked excitedly about what had happened the night before.

'Mother says will you come and spend the day with us?' said Alec. 'Do come. You'll like Mother, she's a dear.'

The two boys went back to Sea Cottage. The girls welcomed them, and Mother shook hands with Ben very politely.

'I'm glad you can come for the day,' she said. 'You'd better go up to the girls' bedroom and play there. I want the sitting-room to do some writing in this morning.'

So they all went up to the bedroom above, and sat down to talk. 'It's nice of Mother to send us up here,' said Hilary. 'We can talk in peace. What are our plans for Thursday, captain?'

'Well, I don't quite know,' said Ben slowly. 'You see, we've got to be there at midnight, haven't we? – but we simply must be there a good time before that, because of the tide. You see, we can't get into either cave if the tide is up. We'd be dashed to pieces.'

The children stared at Smuggler Ben in dismay. None of them had thought of that.

'What time would we have to be there?' asked Alec.

'We'd have to be there about half-past nine, as far as I can reckon,' said Ben. 'Can you leave by that time? What would your mother say?'

'Mother wouldn't let us, I'm sure of that,' said Hilary in disappointment. 'She was so dreadfully worried about us last night. I'm quite sure if we told her what we wanted to do, she would say "no" at once.'

'She isn't in bed by that time, then?' said Ben.

The children shook their heads. All four were puzzled and disappointed. They couldn't think how to get over the difficulty. There was no way out of the cottage except through the sitting-room door – and Mother would be in the room, writing or reading, at the time they wanted to go out. 'What about getting out of the window?' said Alec, going over to look. But that was quite impossible, too. It was too far to jump, and, anyway, Mother would be sure to hear any noise they made.

'It looks as if I'll have to go alone,' said Ben gloomily. 'It's funny – I used to like doing everything all by myself, you know – but I don't like it now at all. I want to be with my three men!'

'Oh, Ben – it would be awful thinking of you down in those caves finding out what was happening – and us in our beds, wanting and longing to be with you!' cried Hilary.

'Well, I simply don't know what else to do,' said Ben. 'If you can't come, you can't. And certainly I wouldn't let you come after your mother had gone to bed, because by that time the tide would be up, and you'd simply be washed away as soon as you set foot on the beach. No – I'll go alone – and I'll come and tell you what's happened the next morning.'

The children felt terribly disappointed and gloomy. 'Let's go downstairs into the little study place that's lined with books,' said Hilary, at last. 'I looked into one of the books the other day, and it seemed to be all about this district in the old days. Maybe we might find some bits about smugglers.'

Ben brightened up at once. 'That would be fine,' he said. 'I know Professor Rondel was supposed to have a heap of books about this district. He was a funny man – never talked to anyone. I didn't like him.'

The children went downstairs. Mother called out to them: 'Where are you going?'

'Into the book room,' said Hilary, opening the sitting-room door. 'We may, mayn't we?'

'Yes, but be sure to take care of any book you use, and put it back into its right place,' said Mother. They promised this and then went into the little study.

'My word! What hundreds of books!' said Ben

in amazement. The walls were lined with them, almost from floor to ceiling. The boy ran his eyes along the shelves. He picked out a book and looked at it.

'Here's a book about the moors behind here,' he said. 'And maps, too. Look – I've been along here – and crossed that stream just there.'

The children looked. 'We ought to go for some walks with you over those lovely moors, Ben,' said Alec. 'I'd like that.'

Hilary took down one or two books and looked through them, too, trying to find something exciting to read. She found nothing and put them back. Frances showed her a book on the top shelf.

'Look,' she said, 'do you think that would be any good? It's called *Old-Time Smugglers' Haunts*.'

'It might be interesting,' said Hilary, and stood on a chair to get the book. It was big and old and smelt musty. The girl jumped down with it and opened it on the table. The first picture she saw made her cry out.

'Oh, look – here's an old picture of this village! Here are the cliffs – and there are the old, old houses that the fishermen still live in!'

She was quite right. Underneath the picture was written: 'A little-known smugglers' haunt. See page 66.'

They turned to page sixty-six, and found

printed there an account of the caves in the little cove on the beach. 'The best-known smuggler of those days was a dark, fiery man named Smuggler Ben,' said the book. The children exclaimed in surprise and looked at Ben.

'How funny!' they cried. 'Did you know that, Ben?'

'No,' said Ben. 'My name is really Benjamin, of course, but everyone calls me Ben. I'm dark, too. I wonder if Smuggler Ben was an ancestor of mine — you know, some sort of relation a hundred or more years ago?'

'Quite likely,' said Alec. 'I wish we could find a picture of him to see if he's like you.'

But they couldn't. They turned over the pages of the book and gave it up. But before they shut it Ben took hold of it. He had an idea.

'I wonder if by chance there's a mention of that blocked-up passage,' he said. 'It would be fun to know where it comes out, wouldn't it?'

He looked carefully through the book. He came again to page sixty-six, and looked at it closely. 'Someone has written a note in the margin of this page,' he said, holding it up to the light. 'It's written in pencil, very faintly. I can hardly make it out.'

The children did make it out at last. 'For more information, see page 87 of *Days of Smugglers*,' the note said. The children looked at one another.

'That would be a book,' said Alec, moving to the shelves. 'Let's see who can find it first.'

Hilary found it. She was always the sharpest of the three. It was a small book, bound in black, and the print was rather faded. She turned to page eighty-seven. The book was all about the district they were staying in, and on page eighty-seven was a description of the old caves. And then came something that excited the children very much. 'Read it out, Ben, read it out!' cried Alec. 'It's important.'

So Ben read it out. '"From a well-hidden opening between two old smugglers' caves is a curious passage, partly natural, partly man-made, probably by the smugglers themselves. This runs steadily upwards through the cliffs, and eventually stops not far from a little stream. A well-hidden hole leads upwards on to the moor. This was probably the way the smugglers used when they took their goods from the caves, over the country."'

The children stared at one another, trembling with excitement. 'So that's where the passage goes to!' said Alec. 'My word – if only we could find the other end! Ben, have you any idea at all where it ends?'

'None at all,' said Ben. 'But it wouldn't be very difficult to find out! We know whereabouts the beginnings of the passage are – and if we

follow a more or less straight line inland till we
come to a stream on the moors, we might be able
to spot the hole!'

'I say! Let's go now, at once, this very minute!' cried Hilary, shouting in her excitement.

'Shut up, silly,' said Alec. 'Do you want to tell everyone our secrets? It's almost dinnertime. We can't go now. But I vote we go immediately afterwards!'

'Professor Rondel must have known all about those caves,' said Ben thoughtfully. 'I suppose he couldn't have anything to do with the strange people we overheard last night? No – that's too far-fetched. But the whole thing is very strange. I do hope we shall be able to find the entrance to the other end of that secret passage.'

Mother called the children at that moment. 'Dinner!' she cried. 'Come along, bookworms, and have a little something to eat.'

They were all hungry. They went to wash and make themselves tidy, and then sat down and ate a most enormous meal. Ben liked the children's mother very much. She talked and laughed, and he didn't feel a bit shy of her.

'You know, Alec and the girls really thought you were going after them with that knife of yours,' she said.

Ben went red. 'I did feel rather fierce that day,' he said. 'But it's awful when people come and spoil your secret places, isn't it? Now I'm glad they came, because they're the first friends I've ever had. We're having a fine time.'

Mother looked out of the window as the children finished up the last of the jam tarts.

'It's clearing up,' she said. 'I think you all ought to go out. It will be very wet underfoot but you can put on your wellingtons. Why don't you go out on the moors for a change?'

'Oh *yes*, we will!' cried all four children at once. Mother was rather astonished.

'Well, you don't usually welcome any suggestions of walking in the wet,' she said. 'I believe you've got some sort of secret plan!'

But nobody told her what it was!

CHAPTER 7

GOOD HUNTING

After dinner the children put on their boots and macs. They pulled on their sou'westers, and said goodbye to their mother, and set off.

'Now for a good old hunt,' said Ben. 'First let's go to the cliff that juts over my little cove. Then we'll try to make out where the passage begins underground and set off from that spot.'

It wasn't long before they were over the cove. The wind whipped their faces, and overhead the clouds scudded by. Ben went to about the middle of the cliff over the cove and stood there.

'I should say that the blocked-up passage runs roughly under here,' he said. 'Now let's think. Does it run quite straight from where it begins? It curves a bit, doesn't it?'

'Yes, but it soon curved back again to the blocked-up part,' said Alec eagerly. 'So you can

307

count it about straight to there. Let's walk in a straight line from here till we think we've come over the blocked-up bit.'

They walked over the cliff inland, foot-deep in purple-heather. Then Ben stopped. 'I reckon we must just about be over the blocked-up bit,' he said. 'Now listen – we've got to look for a stream. There are four of us. We'll all part company and go off in different directions to look for the stream. Give a yell if you find one.'

Soon Alec gave a yell. 'There's a kind of stream here! It runs along for a little way and then disappears into a sort of little gully. I expect it makes its way down through the cliff some-where and springs out into the sea. Would this be the stream, do you think?'

Everyone ran to where Alec stood. Ben looked down at the little brown rivulet. It was certainly very small.

'It's been bigger once upon a time,' he said, pointing to where the bed was dry and wide. 'Maybe this is the one. There doesn't seem to be another, anyway.'

'We'll hunt about around here for an open-ing of some sort,' said Alec, his face red with excitement.

They all hunted about, and it was Hilary who found it – quite by accident!

She was walking over the heather, her eyes

glancing round for any hole, when her foot went right through into space! She had trodden on what she thought was good solid ground, over which heather grew – but almost at once she sank on one knee as her foot went through some sort of hole!

'I say! My foot's gone through a hole here,' she yelled. 'Is it the one? It went right through it. I nearly sprained my ankle.'

The others came up. Ben pulled Hilary up and then parted the heather to see. Certainly a big hole was there – and certainly it seemed to go down a good way.

The children tugged away at armfuls of heather and soon got the tough roots out. The sides of the hole fell away as they took out the heather. Ben switched his torch on when it was fairly large. There seemed to be quite a big drop down.

'We'd better slide down a rope,' he said.

'We haven't got one,' said Alec.

'I've got one round my waist,' said Ben, and undid a piece of strong rope from under his red belt. A stout gorse bush stood not far off, and Ben wound it round the strong stem at the bottom, pricking himself badly but not seeming to feel it at all.

'I'll go down,' he said. He took hold of the rope and lay down on the heather. Then he put his legs into the hole and let himself go, holding tightly to the rope. He slid into the hole, and went a good way down.

'See anything?' yelled Alec.

'Yes. There *is* an underground channel here of some sort!' came Ben's voice, rather muffled. 'I believe we're on to the right one. Wait a minute. I'm going to kick away a bit with my feet, and get some of the loose soil away.'

After a bit Ben's voice came again, full of excitement.

'Come on down! There's a kind of underground channel, worn away by water. I reckon a stream must have run here at some time.'

One by one the excited children slipped down the rope. They found what Ben had said – a kind of underground channel or tunnel plainly made by water of some kind in far-off days. Ben had his torch and the others had theirs. They switched them on.

Ben led the way. It was a curious path to take. Sometimes the roof was so low that the children had to crouch down, and once they had to go on hands and knees. Ben showed them the marks of tools in places where rocks jutted into the channel.

'Those marks were made by the smugglers, I reckon,' he said. 'They found this way and made it into a usable passage. They must have found it difficult getting some of their goods along here.'

'I expect they unpacked those boxes we saw and carried the goods on their backs in bags or sacks,' said Frances, seeing the picture clearly in her mind. 'Ooooh – isn't it strange to think that heaps of smugglers have gone up this dark passage carrying smuggled goods years and years ago!'

They went on for a good way and then suddenly came to an impassable bit where the roof had fallen in. They stopped.

'Well, here we are,' said Ben, 'we've come to the blocked-up part once more. Now the thing is – how far along is it blocked-up – just a few yards, easy to clear – or a quarter of a mile?'

'I don't see how we can tell,' said Alec. The four children stood and looked at the fallen stones and soil. It was most annoying to think they could get no further.

'I know!' said Hilary suddenly. 'I know! One of us could go in at the other end of the passage and yell. Then, if we can hear anything, we shall know the blockage isn't stretching very far!'

'Good idea, Hilary,' said Ben, pleased. 'Yes, that really *is* a good idea. I'd better be the one to go because I can go quickly. It'll take me a little time, so you must be patient. I shall yell loudly when I get up to the blocked bit, and then I shall knock on some stones with my spade. We did leave the spades there, didn't we?'

'We did,' said Alec. 'I say – this is getting awfully exciting, isn't it?'

Ben squeezed past the others and made his way up the channel. He climbed up the rope and sped off over the heather to the cliff side. Down the narrow path he went, and jumped down into the cove.

Meanwhile, the others had sat down in the tunnel, to wait patiently for any noise they might hear.

'It will be terribly disappointing if we don't hear anything,' said Frances. They waited and waited. It seemed ages to them.

And then suddenly they heard something! It was Ben's voice, rather muffled and faint, but still quite unmistakable: 'Helloooooooooo! Helloooooooooo!'

Then came the sharp noise of a spade on rock: Crack! Crack! Crack!

'Helloooooooooooo!' yelled back all three children, wildly excited. 'Helloooooooooo!'

'Come – and – join – me!' yelled Ben's voice. 'Come – and – join – me!'

'Coming, coming, coming!' shouted Alec, Hilary and Frances, and all three scrambled back up to the entrance of the hole, swarming up the rope like monkeys.

They tore over the heather back to the cliff side and almost fell down the steep path. Down into the cove on the sand – in the big cave – up on to the ledge – up the nail-studded hole – out on the ledge in the enormous cave – down to the rocky floor – over to the passage between the two caves – up the wall – and into the blocked-up passage where Ben was impatiently waiting for them.

'You *have* been quick,' he cried. 'I say – I could hear your voices quite well. The blocked piece can't stretch very far. Isn't that good? Do you feel able to tackle it hard now? If so, I believe we might clear it.'

'I could tackle anything!' said Alec, taking off his mac. 'I could tackle the cliff itself!'

Everyone laughed. They were all pleased and excited, and felt able to do anything, no matter how hard it was.

'What's the time?' suddenly said Alec, when they had worked hard for a time, loosening the soil and filling the sacks. 'Mother's expecting us in to tea, you know.'

'It's quarter-past four already,' said Hilary in dismay. 'We must stop. But we'll come back after tea.'

They sped off to their tea, and Mother had to cut another big plateful of bread and butter because they finished up every bit. Then off they went again, back to their exciting task.

'I say, I say, I say!' suddenly cried Alec, making everyone jump. 'I've just thought of something marvellous.'

'What?' asked everyone curiously.

'Well – if we can get this passage clear, we can come down it on Thursday night, from outside,' said Alec. 'We don't need to bother about the tides or anything. We can slip out at half-past eleven, go to the entrance on the moor and come down here and see what's happening!'

'Gosh! I never thought of that!' cried Hilary.

Ben grinned. 'That's fine,' he said. 'Yes – you can easily do that. You needn't disturb your mother at all. I think I'd better be here earlier, though, in case those people change their plans and come before they say. Though I don't think they will, because if they come in by motorboat they'll need high tide to get their boat into the long cave.'

The children went on working at the passage. Suddenly Ben gave a shout of joy.

'We're through! My spade went right through into nothing just then! Where's my torch?'

He shone it in front of him, and the children saw that he had spoken the truth. The light of the torch shone beyond into the other side of the passage! There was only a small heap of fallen earth to manage now.

'I think we'll finish this,' said Alec, though he knew the girls were tired out. 'I can't leave that little bit till tomorrow! You girls can sit down and have a rest. Ben and I can tackle this last bit.

It will be easy.'

It was. Before another half-hour had gone by, the passage was quite clear, and the children were able to walk up and down it from end to end. They felt pleased with themselves.

'Now we'll have to wait till Thursday,' sighed Alec. 'Gosh, what a long time it is – a whole day and a night and then another whole day. I simply can't wait!'

But they had to. They met Ben the next day and planned everything. They could hardly go to sleep on Wednesday night, and when Thursday dawned they were all awake as early as the sun.

CHAPTER 8
THURSDAY EVENING

The day seemed very long indeed to the children – but they had a lovely surprise in the afternoon. Their father arrived, and with him he brought their Uncle Ned. Mother rushed to the gate to meet them as soon as she saw them, and the children shouted for joy.

Uncle Ned said he could stay a day or two, and Daddy said he would stay for a whole week.

'Where's Uncle Ned going to sleep?' asked Alec. 'In my room?'

In the ordinary way the boy would have been very pleased at the idea of his uncle sleeping in the same room with him – but tonight a grown-up might perhaps spoil things.

'Ned will have to sleep on the sofa in the sit-ting-room,' said Mother. 'I don't expect he will mind. He's had worse places to sleep in this war!'

Both Daddy and Uncle Ned were in the

317

Army. It was lucky they had leave just when the children were on holiday. They could share a bit of it, too! All the children were delighted.

'I say – how are we going to slip out at half-past eleven tonight if Uncle Ned is sleeping in the sitting-room?' said Hilary, when they were alone. 'We shall have to be jolly careful not to wake him!'

'Well, there's nothing for it but to creep through to the door,' said Alec. 'And if he does wake, we'll have to beg him not to tell tales of us.'

The night came at last. The children went to bed as usual, but not one of them could go to sleep. They lay waiting for the time to pass, and it passed so slowly that once or twice Hilary thought her watch must have stopped, but it hadn't.

At last half-past eleven came – the time when they had arranged to leave, to go to meet Ben in the passage above the caves. Very quietly the children dressed. They all wore shorts, jerseys, their smugglers' hats, sashes and rubber boots. They stole down the stairs very softly. Not a stair creaked, not a child coughed.

The door of the sitting-room was a little open. Alec pushed it a little further and put his head in. The room was dark. On the sofa Uncle Ned was lying, his regular breathing telling the children that he was asleep.

'He's asleep,' whispered Alec, in a low voice. 'I'll go across first and open the door. Then you two step across quietly to me. I'll shut the door after us.'

The boy went across the room to the door. He opened it softly. He had already oiled it that day, by Ben's orders, and it made no sound. A streak of moonlight came in.

Silently the three children passed out and Alec shut the door. Just as they were going through the door, their uncle woke. He opened his eyes – and to his very great amazement saw the figures of the three children going quietly out of the open door. Then it shut.

Uncle Ned sat up with a jerk. Could he be dreaming? He opened the door and looked out. No – he wasn't dreaming. There were the three figures hurrying along to the moor in the moonlight. Uncle Ned was more astonished than he had ever been in his life before.

'Now what in the world do these kids think they are doing?' he wondered. 'Little monkeys slipping out like this just before midnight. What are they up to? I'll go after them and see. Maybe they'll let me join in their prank, whatever it is. Anyway, Alec oughtn't to take his two sisters out at this time of night!'

Uncle Ned pulled on a mackintosh over his pyjamas and set out down the lane after the children. They had no idea he was some way behind them. They were thrilled because they thought they had got out so easily without being heard!

They got to the hole in the heather and by the light of their torch slid down the rope. Uncle Ned was more and more amazed as he saw one child after another slide down and disappear completely. He didn't know any hole was there, of course. He found it after a time and decided to go down it himself.

Meanwhile, the children were half-way down the passage. There they met Ben, and whispered in excitement to him. 'We got out without being seen – though our uncle was sleeping on the sofa near the door! Ben, have you seen or heard anything yet?'

'Not a thing,' said Ben. 'But they should be here soon, because it's almost midnight and the tide is full.'

They all went down to the end of the passage, and jumped down to stand at the end of the long, narrow cave. This was now full of water, and the waves rushed up it continually.

'Easy enough to float any motorboat right in,' said Ben. 'I wonder what they're bringing.'

'Listen!' said Hilary suddenly. 'I'm sure I can hear something.'

'It's the chug-chug of that motorboat again,' whispered Alec, a shiver going down his back.

He wasn't frightened, but it was all so exciting he couldn't help trembling. The girls were the same. Their knees shook a little. Only Ben was quite still and fearless.

'Now don't switch your torches on by mistake, for goodness' sake,' whispered Ben, as the chugging noise came nearer. 'We'll stay here till we see the boat coming into the long channel of this cave then we'll hop up into the passage and listen hard.'

The motorboat came nearer and nearer. Then as it nosed gently into the long cave with its deep inlet of water, the engine was shut off.

'Now we must go,' said Ben, and the four children turned. They climbed up into the passage above the caves and stood there, listening.

People got out of the motorboat, which was apparently tied up to some rock. Torches were switched on. Ben, who was leaning over the hole from the passage, counted three people going into the big cave – two men and a woman. One of the men seemed somehow familiar to him, but he was gone too quickly for Ben to take a second look.

'Well here we are,' said a voice from the enormous cave below. 'I will leave you food and drink, and you will wait here till it is safe to go inland. You have maps to show you how to go. You know what to do. Do it well. Come back here and the motorboat will fetch you a week from now.'

The children listening above could not make out at all what was happening. Who were the people? And what were the two of them to do? Alec pressed hard by Ben to listen better. His foot touched a pebble and set it rolling down into the space between the caves. Before he could stop himself he gave a low cry of annoyance.

There was instant silence in the cave. Then the first voice spoke again very sharply: 'What was that? Did you hear anything?'

A wave roared up the narrow cave nearby and made a great noise. Whilst the splashing was going on Ben whispered to Alec: 'Move back up the passage, quick! You idiot, they heard you! They'll be looking for us in a minute!'

The children hurried back along the passage as quietly as they could, their hearts beating painfully. And half-way along it they bumped into somebody!

Hilary screamed. Frances almost fainted with fright. Then the somebody took their arms and said: 'Now what in the world are you kids doing here at this time of night?'

'Uncle Ned, oh, Uncle Ned!' said Hilary in a faint voice. 'Oh, it's marvellous to have a grown-up just at this very minute to help us! Uncle Ned, something very strange is going on. Tell him, Alec.'

Alec told his astonished uncle very quickly all that had happened. He listened without a word and then spoke in a sharp, stern voice that the children had never heard before.

'They're spies! They've come over from the coast of Ireland. It's just opposite here, you know. Goodness knows what they're going to do – some dirty work, I expect. We've got to stop them. Now let me think. How can we get them? Can they get away from the caves except by motorboat?'

'Only up this passage, until the tide goes down,' said Ben. 'Sir – listen to me. I could slip down the hole and cast off the motorboat by myself. I know how to start it up. I believe I could do it. Then you could hold this passage, couldn't you, and send Alec and the girls back to get their father. You'd have to get somebody to keep guard outside the cave as soon as the tide goes down, in case they try to escape round the cliffs.'

'Leave that to me,' said Uncle Ned grimly. 'Can you really get away in that motorboat? If you can, you'll take their only means of escape. Well, go and try. Good luck to you. You're a brave lad!'

Ben winked at the others, who were staring at him open-mouthed. Then he slipped along down the passage again until he came to the opening.

He stood there listening before he let himself down into the space between the caves. It was plain that the people there had come to the conclusion that the noise they had heard was nothing to worry about, for they were talking together. There was the clink of glasses as the boy dropped down quietly to the floor below the passage.

'They're wishing each other good luck!' said the boy to himself, with a grin. He went to the motorboat, which was gently bobbing up and down as waves ran under it up the inlet of water in the cave. He climbed quietly in. He felt about for the rope that was tied round a rock, and slipped it loose. The next wave took the boat down with it, and as soon as he dared, Ben started up the engine to take her out of the deep channel in the cave.

He was lucky in getting the boat out fairly quickly. As soon as the engine started up, there came a shout from the cave, and Ben knew that the two men there had run to see what was happening. He ducked in case there was any shooting. He guessed that the men would be desperate when they saw their boat going.

He got the boat clear, and swung her out on the water that filled the cove. The boy knew the coast almost blindfolded, and soon the little motorboat was chug-chug-chugging across the

open sea towards the beach where a little jetty ran out, and where Ben could tie her up. He was filled with glee. It was marvellous to think he had beaten those men – and that woman, too, whoever she was. Spies! Well – now they knew what British boys and girls could do!

He wondered what the others were doing. He felt certain that Alec and the girls were even now speeding up the passage, climbing out through the heather and racing back home to wake their father.

And that is exactly what they *were* doing! They had left their uncle in the passage – and in his hand was his loaded revolver. No one could escape by that passage, even if they knew of it.

'Tell your father what you have told me, and tell him Ben has taken the boat away,' he said. 'I want men to guard the outer entrance of the caves as soon as the tide goes down. I'll remain here to guard this way of escape. Go quickly!'

CHAPTER 9

THINGS MOVE QUICKLY

Alec and the two girls left their uncle and stumbled up the dark passage, lighting their way by their small torches. All three were trembling with excitement. It seemed suddenly a very serious thing that was happening. Spies! Who would have thought of that?

They went on up the passage. Soon they came to the place where the roof fell very low indeed, and down they went on their hands and knees to crawl through the low tunnel.

'I don't like that bit much,' said Frances, when they were through it. 'I shall dream about that! Come on – we can stand upright again now. Whatever do you suppose Daddy and Mother will say?'

'I can't imagine,' said Alec. 'All I know is that it's a very lucky thing for us that Daddy and Uncle happened to be here now. Gosh – didn't I

327

jump when we bumped into Uncle Ned in this passage!'

'I screamed,' said Hilary, rather ashamed of herself. 'But honestly I simply couldn't help it. It was awful to bump into somebody strange like that in the darkness. But wasn't I glad when I heard Uncle Ned's voice!'

'Here we are at last,' said Alec, as they came to where the rope hung down the hole. 'I'll go up first and then give you two girls a hand. Give me a heave, Hilary.'

Hilary heaved him up and he climbed the rope quickly, hand over hand, glad that he had been so good at gym at school. You never knew when things would come in useful!

He lay down on the heather and helped the girls up. They stood out on the moor in the moonlight, getting back their breath, for it wasn't easy to haul themselves up the rope.

'Now come on,' said Hilary. 'We haven't any time to lose. I shouldn't be surprised if those spies know about the passage and make up their minds to try it. We don't want to leave Uncle Ned too long. After all, it's three against one.'

They tore over the heather, and came to the sandy lane where Sea Cottage shone in the moonlight. They went in at the open door and made their way to their parents' bedroom. Alec hammered on the door, and then went in.

His father and mother were sitting up in astonishment. They switched on the light and stared at the three children, all fully dressed as they were.

'What's the meaning of this?' asked their father. But before he could say a word more the three children began to pour out their story. At first their parents could not make out what they were talking about, and their mother made the girls stop talking so that Alec could tell the tale.

'But this is unbelievable!' said their father, dressing as quickly as possible. 'Simply unbelievable! Is Ned really down a secret passage, holding three spies at bay? And Ben has gone off with their motorboat? Am I dreaming?'

'No, Daddy, you're not,' said Alec. 'It's all quite true. We kept everything a secret till tonight, because secrets are such fun. We didn't know that anything serious was up till tonight, really. Are you going to get help?'

'I certainly am,' said Daddy. He went to the telephone downstairs and was soon on to the nearest military camp. He spoke to a most surprised commanding officer, who listened in growing amazement.

'So you must send a few men over as quickly as possible,' said Daddy. 'The children say there are three men in the caves — or rather, two men and one woman — but there may be more, of course – and more may arrive. We can't tell. Hurry, won't you?'

He put down the receiver of the telephone and turned to look at the waiting children. 'Now let me see,' he said thoughtfully. 'I shall want one of you to take me to where Ned is, and I must leave someone behind to guide the soldiers down to the cove. They must be there to guard the entrance to the caves, so that if the spies try to escape by the beach, they will find they can't. Alec, you had better come with me. Frances and Hilary, you can go with Mother and the soldiers, when they come, and show them the way down the cliff and the entrance to the caves. Come along, Alec.'

The two set off. Alec talked hard all the way, for there was a great deal to tell. His father listened in growing astonishment. Really, you never knew what children were doing half the time!

'I suppose your mother thought you were playing harmless games of smugglers,' he said, 'and all the time you were on the track of dangerous spies! Well, well, well!'

'We didn't really know they were spies till tonight,' said Alec honestly. 'It was all a game at first. Look, Daddy – here's the hole. We have to slide down this rope.'

'This really is a weird adventure,' said his

father, and down the rope he went. Alec followed him. Soon they were standing beside Uncle Ned, who was still in the passage, his revolver in his hand.

'There's been a lot of excited talking,' he said in a low voice to his brother, 'and I think they've been trying to find a way out. But the tide is still very high, and they daren't walk out on the sand yet. If they don't know of this passage, they won't try it, of course – but we'd better stay here in case they do. When are the soldiers coming?'

'At once,' said Daddy. 'I've left the two girls behind to guide them down to the cove. Then they will hide, and guard the entrance to the caves, that is as soon as the tide goes down enough.'

'Do the spies know you're here, Uncle Ned?' asked Alec, in a low voice.

'No,' said his uncle. 'They know someone has gone off with their motorboat, but that's all they know. What about creeping down to the end of the passage to see if we can overhear anything? They might drop a few secrets!'

The three of them crept down to the end of the passage, and leaned out over the hole that led down to the space between the two caves. They could hear the waves still washing up the narrow channel in the long cave.

The two men and the woman were talking

angrily. 'Who could have known we were here? Someone has given the game away! No one but ourselves and the other three knew what we were planning to do.'

'Is there no other way out?' said a man's impatient voice, very deep and foreign. 'Rondel, you know all these caves and passages – or so you said. How did the old smugglers get their goods away? There must have been a land path they used.'

'There was,' said the other man. 'There is a passage above this cave that leads on to the moors. But as far as I know it is completely blocked up.'

'As far as you know!' said the other man, in a scornful voice. 'Haven't you found out? What do you suppose you are paid for, Rondel? Aren't you paid for letting us know any well-hidden caves on this coast? Where is this passage? Do you know?'

'Yes, I know,' said Rondel. 'It's above this one, and the entrance to it is just between this cave and the one we used for the motorboat. We have to climb up a little way. I've never been up it myself, because I heard it was blocked up by a roof-fall years ago. But we can try it and see.'

'We'd better get back up the passage a bit,' whispered Alec's father. 'If they come up here, we may have trouble. Get on to that bit where the big rock juts out and the passage goes round it. We can get behind that and give them a scare. They'll shoot if they see us. I don't want to shoot if I can help it, for I've a feeling they will be more useful alive than dead!'

Very silently the three went back up the passage to where a rock jutted out and the way went round it. They crouched down behind the rock and waited, their torches switched off. Alec heard their breathing and it sounded very loud. But they had to breathe! He wondered if Daddy and Uncle could hear his heart beating, because it seemed to make a very loud thump just then!

Meanwhile, the three spies were trying to find the entrance to the passage. Rondel had a powerful torch, and he soon found the hole that led to the ledge where the secret passage began.

'Here it is!' he said. 'Look – we can easily get up there. I'll go first.'

Alec heard a scrambling noise as the man climbed up. Then he pulled up the other two. They all switched on their torches and the dark passage was lit up brightly.

'It seems quite clear,' said the other man. 'I should think we could escape this way. You go ahead, Rondel. We'll follow. I can't see any sign of it being blocked up, I must say! This is a bit of luck.'

They went on up the passage, talking. They

went slowly, and Alec and the others could hear their footsteps and voices coming gradually nearer. Alec's heart beat painfully and he kept swallowing something in his throat. The excitement was almost too much for him to bear.

The three spies came almost up to the jutting-out rock. And then they got the shock of their lives! Alec's father spoke in a loud stern voice that made Alec jump.

'Halt! Come another step, and we'll shoot!'

The spies halted at once in a panic. They switched off their torches.

'Who's there?' came Rondel's voice.

Nobody answered. The spies talked together in low voices and decided to go back the way they had come. They were not risking going round that rock! They didn't know how many people were there. It was plain that somebody knew of their plans and meant to capture them.

Alec heard the three making their way quietly back down the passage.

'Daddy! I expect they think the tide will soon be going down and they hope to make their escape by way of the beach,' whispered Alec. 'I hope the soldiers will be there in time.'

'Don't you worry about that!' said his father. 'As soon as the tide washes off the beach, it will be full of soldiers.'

'I wish I could be there,' said Alec longingly.

'I don't expect the spies will come up here again.'

'Well, you can go and see what's happening if you like,' said Daddy. 'Your uncle and I will stay here – but you can see if the soldiers have arrived and if the girls are taking them down to the cove.'

Alec was delighted. More excitement for him, after all! He went up the passage and swarmed up the rope out of the entrance-hole. He sped over the moor to the cottage.

But no one was there. It was quite empty. 'I suppose the soldiers have arrived and Mother and the girls have taken them to the cove,' thought Alec. 'Yes – there are big wheel-marks in the road – a lorry has been here. Oh – there it is, in the shade of those trees over there. I'd better hurry or I'll miss the fun!'

Off he dashed to the cliff edge, and down the narrow, steep path. Where were the others? Waiting in silence down on the beach? Alec nearly fell down the steep path trying to hurry! What an exciting night!

CHAPTER 10

THE END OF IT ALL

Just as Alec was scrambling down the steep cliff, he heard the sound of a low voice from the top. 'Is that you, Alec?'

Alec stopped. It was Ben's voice. 'Ben!' he whispered in excitement. 'Come on down. You're just in time. How did you get here?'

Ben scrambled down beside him. 'I thought it was you,' he said. 'I saw you going over the edge of the cliff as I came up the lane. What's happened?'

Alec told him. Ben listened in excitement.

'So they know there's someone in the secret passage,' he said. 'They'll just have to try to escape by the beach then! Well, they'll be over-powered there, no doubt about that. I tied up the motorboat by the jetty, Alec. It's a real beauty – small but very powerful. It's got a lovely engine. Then I raced back to see if I could be in at the end.'

337

'Well, you're just in time,' said Alec. 'I'm going to hop down on to the beach now and see where the others are.'

'Be careful,' Ben warned him. 'The soldiers won't know it's you, and may take a pot shot at you.'

That scared Alec. He stopped before he jumped down on to the sand.

'Well, I think maybe we'd better stay here then,' he said. 'We can see anything that happens from here, can't we? Look, the tide is going down nicely now. Where do you suppose the others are, Ben?'

'I should think they are somewhere on the rocks that run round the cove,' said Ben, looking carefully round. 'Look, Alec – there's something shining just over there – see? I guess that's a gun. We can't see the man holding it – but the moonlight just picks out a shiny bit of his gun.'

'I hope the girls and Mother are safe,' said Alec.

'You may be sure they are,' said Ben. 'I wonder what the three spies are doing now. I guess they are waiting till the tide is low enough for them to come out.'

At that very moment Rondel was looking out of the big cave to see if it was safe to try and escape over the beach. He was not going to try to go up the cliff path, for he felt sure there would be someone at the top. Their only hope lay in slipping round the corner of the cove and making their way up the cliff some way off. Rondel knew the coast by heart, and if he only had the chance he felt certain he could take the others to safety.

The tide was going down rapidly. The sand was very wet and shone in the moonlight. Now and again a big wave swept up the beach, but the power behind it was gone. It could not dash anyone against the rocks now. Rondel turned to his two companions and spoke to them in a low voice.

'Now's our chance. We shall have to try the beach whilst our enemies think the tide is still high. Take hold of Gretel's hand, Otto, in case a wave comes. Follow me. Keep as close to the cliff as possible in case there is a watcher above.'

The three of them came silently out of the big cave. Its entrance lay in darkness and they looked like deep black shadows as they moved quietly to the left of the cave. They made their way round the rocks, stopping as a big wave came splashing up the smooth sand. It swept round their feet, but no higher. Then it ran back down the sand again to the sea, and the three moved on once more.

Then a voice rang out in the moonlight: 'We have you covered! There is no escape this way! Hands up!'

Rondel had his revolver in his hand in a moment and guns glinted in the hands of the others, too. But they did not know where their enemies were. The rocks lay in black shadows, and no one could be seen.

'There are men all round this cove,' said the voice. 'You cannot escape. Put your hands up and surrender. Throw your revolvers down, please.'

Rondel spoke to the others in a savage voice. He was in a fierce rage, for all his plans were ruined. It seemed as if he were urging the others to fight. But they were wiser than Rondel. The other man threw his revolver down on the sand and put his hands above his head. The woman did the same. They glinted there like large silver shells.

'Hands up, you!' commanded a voice. Rondel shouted something angry in a foreign language and then threw his gun savagely at the nearest rocks. It hit them and the trigger was struck. The revolver went off with a loud explosion that echoed round and round the little cove and made everyone, Rondel as well, jump violently.

'Stand where you are,' said a voice. And out from the shadow of the rocks came a soldier in the uniform of an officer. He walked up to the three spies and had a look at them. He felt them all over to see if there were any more weapons hidden about them. There were none.

He called to his men. 'Come and take them.'

Four men stepped out from the rocks around the cove. Alec and Ben leapt down on to the sand. Mother and the two girls came out from their hiding-place in a small cave. Ben ran up to the spies. He peered into the face of one of the men.

'I know who this is!' he cried. 'It's Professor Rondel, who lived in Sea Cottage. I've seen him hundreds of times! He didn't have many friends – only two or three men who came to see him sometimes.'

'Oh,' said the officer, staring with interest at Ben. 'Well, we'll be very pleased to know who the two or three men were. You'll be very useful to us, my boy. Now then – quick march! Up the cliff we go and into the lorry! The sooner we get these three into a safe place the better.'

Alec's father and uncle appeared at that moment. They had heard the sound of the shot when Rondel's revolver struck the rock and went off, and they had come to see what was happening. Alec ran to them and told them.

'Good work!' said Daddy. 'Three spies caught – and maybe the others they work with, too, if Ben can point them out. Good old Smuggler Ben!'

The three spies were put into the lorry and the driver climbed up behind the wheel. The officer saluted and took his place. Then the lorry rumbled off into the moonlit night. The four children watched it go, their eyes shining.

'This is the most thrilling night I've ever had in my life,' said Alec, with a sigh. 'I don't suppose I'll ever have a more exciting one, however long I live. Gosh, my heart did beat fast when we were hiding in the cave. It hurt me.'

'Same here,' said Hilary. 'Oh, Daddy – you didn't guess what you were in for, did you, when you came home yesterday?'

'I certainly didn't,' said Daddy, putting his arm round the two girls and pushing them towards the house. 'Come along – you'll all be tired out. It must be nearly dawn!'

'Back to Professor Rondel's own house!' said Alec. 'Isn't it funny! He got all his information from his books – and we found some of it there, too. We'll show you if you like, Daddy.'

'Not tonight,' said Daddy firmly. 'Tonight – or rather this morning, for it's morning now – you are going to bed, and to sleep. No more excitement, please! You will have plenty again tomorrow, for you'll have to go over to the police and to the military camp to tell all you know.'

Well, that was an exciting piece of news, too. The children went indoors, Ben with them, for Mother said he had better share Alec's room for the rest of the night.

Soon all four children were in their beds, feeling certain they would never, never be able to go to sleep for one moment.

But it wasn't more than two minutes before they were all sound asleep, as Mother saw when she peeped into the two bedrooms. She went to join Daddy and Uncle Ned.

'Well, I'd simply no idea what the children were doing,' she told them. 'I was very angry with them one night when they came home late because they were caught by the tide when they were exploring those caves. They kept their secret well.'

'They're good kids,' said Daddy, with a yawn. 'Well, let's go to sleep, too. Ned, I hope you'll be able to drop off on the sofa again.'

'I could drop off on the kitchen stove, I'm so tired!' said Ned.

Soon the whole household slept soundly, and did not wake even when the sun came slanting in at the windows. They were all tired out.

They had a late breakfast, and the children chattered nineteen to the dozen as they ate porridge and bacon and eggs. It all seemed amazingly wonderful to them now that it was over. They couldn't help feeling rather proud of themselves.

'I must go,' said Ben, when he had finished an enormous breakfast. 'My uncle is expecting me to go out fishing with him this morning. He'll be angry because I'm late.'

But before Ben could go, a messenger on a motorbike arrived, asking for the four children to go over to the police station at once. The police wanted to know the names of the men with whom Professor Rondel had made friends. This was very important, because unless they knew the names at once, the men might hear of Rondel's capture and fly out of the country.

So off went the four children, and spent a most exciting time telling and retelling their story from the very beginning. The inspector of the police listened carefully, and when everything had been told, and notes taken, he leaned back and looked at the children, his eyes twinkling.

'Well, we have reason to be very grateful to you four smugglers,' he said. 'We shall probably catch the whole nest of spies operating in this part of the country. We suspected it – but we had no idea who the ringleader was. It was Rondel, of course. He was bringing men and women across from Ireland – spies, of course – and taking them about the country either to get information useful to the enemy, or to wreck valuable buildings. He was using the old smugglers' caves to hide his friends in. We shall comb the whole coast now.'

'Can we help you?' asked Ben eagerly. 'I know most of the caves, sir. And we can show you Rondel's books, where all the old caves are described. He's got dozens of them.'

'Good!' said the inspector. 'Well, that's all for today. You will hear from us later. There will be a little reward given to you for services to your country!'

The children filed out, talking excitedly. A little reward! What could it be?

'Sometimes children are given watches as a reward,' said Alec, thinking of a newspaper report he had read. 'We might get a watch each.'

'I hope we don't,' said Hilary, 'because I've already got one – though it doesn't keep very good time.'

But the reward wasn't watches. It was something much bigger than that. Can you possibly guess what it was?

It was the little motorboat belonging to the spies! When the children heard the news, they could hardly believe their ears. But it was quite true. There lay the little motorboat, tied up to the jetty, and on board was a police officer with instructions to hand it over to the four children.

'Oh – thank you!' said Alec, hardly able to speak. 'Thank you very much. Oh, Ben – oh, Ben – isn't it marvellous!'

It *was* marvellous! It was a beautiful little boat

with a magnificent engine. It was called *Otto*.

'That won't do,' said Hilary, looking at the name. 'We'll have that painted out at once. What shall we call our boat? It must be a very good name — something that will remind us of our adventure!'

'I know — I know!' yelled Alec. 'We'll call it *Smuggler Ben*, of course — and good old Ben shall be the captain, and we'll be his crew.'

So *Smuggler Ben* the boat was called, and everyone agreed that it was a really good name. The children have a wonderful time in it. You should see them chug-chugging over the sea at top speed, the spray flying high in the air! Aren't they lucky!